The baby grabbed the ring of Laurie's hand and threw them into the depths of the turbulent Niagara River.

Laurie gasped, looking with disbelief into the white water.

"Morgan," she breathed, "what have you done?"

Cooper Buckingham asked himself the same question as he watched the improbable scene unfold not ten feet away. The woman looked in his direction, straight into Cooper's eyes, as if she'd read his thoughts. The look she gave him might have been a plea for help if it wasn't for the proud tilt of her chin.

And even if she asked, what could he do? He knew nothing about babies, or how to retrieve car keys from the bottom of the Falls—and he had no interest in a devastatingly beautiful blonde with a little red-haired imp in her arms.

Yeah, right.

Dear Reader,

Spring is on the way—and love is blooming in Silhouette Romance this month. To keep his little girl, FABULOUS FATHER Jace McCall needs a pretend bride—fast. Luckily he "proposes" to a woman who doesn't have to pretend to love him in Sandra Steffen's *A Father For Always*.

Favorite author Annette Broadrick continues her bestselling DAUGHTERS OF TEXAS miniseries with *Instant Mommy*, this month's BUNDLES OF JOY selection. Widowed dad Deke Crandall was an expert at raising cattle, but a greenhorn at raising his baby daughter. So when he asked Mollie O'Brien for her help, the marriage-shy rancher had no idea he'd soon be asking for her hand!

In *Wanted: Wife* by Stella Bagwell, handsome Lucas Lowrimore is all set to say "I do," but his number one candidate for a bride has very cold feet. Can he convince reluctant Jenny Prescott to walk those cold feet down the aisle?

Carla Cassidy starts off her new miniseries THE BAKER BROOD with *Deputy Daddy*. Carolyn Baker has to save her infant godchildren from their bachelor guardian, Beau Randolph. After all, what could he know about babies? But then she experienced some of his tender loving care....

And don't miss our other two wonderful books— *Almost Married* by Carol Grace and *The Groom Wore Blue Suede Shoes* by debut author Jessica Travis.

Happy Reading!

Melissa Senate,
Senior Editor

Please address questions and book requests to:
Silhouette Reader Service
U.S.: 3010 Walden Ave., P.O. Box 1325, Buffalo, NY 14269
Canadian: P.O. Box 609, Fort Erie, Ont. L2A 5X3

ALMOST MARRIED

Carol Grace

Silhouette
ROMANCE™
Published by Silhouette Books
America's Publisher of Contemporary Romance

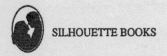

SILHOUETTE BOOKS

ISBN 0-373-19142-1

ALMOST MARRIED

Printed in U.S.A.

Books by Carol Grace

Silhouette Romance

Make Room for Nanny #690
A Taste of Heaven #751
Home Is Where the Heart Is #882
Mail-Order Male #955
The Lady Wore Spurs #1010
*Lonely Millionaire #1057
*Almost A Husband #1105
*Almost Married #1142

*Miramar Inn

CAROL GRACE

has always been interested in travel and living abroad.
She spent her junior year in college in France and
toured the world working on the hospital ship *HOPE*.
She and her husband spent the first year and a half of
their marriage in Iran, where they both taught English.
Then, with their toddler daughter, they lived in Algeria
for two years.

Carol says that writing is another way of making her
life exciting. Her office is an Airstream trailer parked
behind her mountaintop home, which overlooks the
Pacific Ocean and which she shares with her inventor
husband, their daughter, who is now sixteen years old,
and their eleven-year-old son.

LAURIE'S APPLE BAR CAKE

(from Gretel's cookbook)

SERVED AT THE MIRAMAR INN

Ingredients:

1 cup sugar
½ cup soft shortening
1 egg
1½ cups all-purpose flour
½ tsp salt
1½ tsp baking soda
2½ cups peeled and finely chopped apples

Topping:

1 tsp cinnamon
1 cup chopped nuts
⅔ cup firmly packed brown sugar
1 tsp vanilla

Cream sugar with shortening until fluffy; beat in egg. Mix flour with salt and soda into creamed mixture and mix well. Stir in apples. Spread stiff batter evenly in a buttered 10"x15" pan. Sprinkle with mixed topping. Bake at 350°F for 30 minutes. Let cool; cut into bars. Serve with whipped cream or vanilla frozen yogurt. Serves 8.

Chapter One

"Laurie Clayton, meet your goddaughter."

Laurie held out her arms and took from her friend Gretel the most adorable baby she'd ever seen. The baby's little fingers tangled in Laurie's hair and her sweet smell filled her with a bittersweet longing for a child of her own. "Oh, Gret, she's *sooo* cute. A perfect angel."

Gretel sighed. "You wouldn't say that if you'd heard her crying all the way down to the airport. She's teething and it's been awful." Laurie hugged the baby to her and Morgan gurgled happily. "She likes you," Gretel said, then surveyed her friend carefully. "Still slim, gorgeous and single. How come? I thought you'd be the first to take the plunge and have a family. You like kids so much."

"Yes, well, it's still customary to get married first," Laurie said ruefully. "Like you did. Like my sister did."

Gretel nodded understandingly. "You wait here with Morgan. I'll get the car from the garage and bring it around."

Laurie hardly noticed Gretel was gone, she was so entranced with this baby, this miracle of soft skin and round, chubby cheeks. The baby gave her a toothless smile and Laurie thought she'd landed in paradise instead of Buffalo, New York.

"I'll let you get over your jet lag tonight," Gretel promised as they headed out of town into the fertile farmland of upstate New York where Gretel and her husband raised apples, "but tomorrow I'm going to give you the royal tour, from the museum to the zoo and last but not least, Niagara Falls!"

"All in one day?"

Gretel laughed. "We've got five whole days before I join Steve in Seattle. Plenty of time to see everything and let you get to know Morgan. If you're sure you're still up for baby-sitting for two weeks." Gretel shot an anxious glance at her best friend.

Laurie turned her head to smile at her goddaughter. "Of course I'm up for it," she assured Gretel. "I can't wait to have her all to myself. You're right, I've always liked kids. And I adore Morgan already. Her pictures don't do her justice. You don't have to entertain me. I'll be happy to help out around the place. With Steve gone away to school, you must need help picking apples or something."

"We've got a small staff who do the year-round stuff, spraying, grafting, but during harvest a whole crew comes in to work. By that time Steve will be back to oversee the whole thing." She turned to smile at Laurie. "I've been waiting for you so we can relive those carefree days when we were young and foolish, when we flew from coast to coast, flight attendants without a care in the world except which restaurant to go to and which guy to go out with. We'll put Morgan in the back seat with her teething ring and we'll be off."

Laurie noticed Morgan had nodded off and was sleeping peacefully in her car seat, her pale eyelashes dusting her fair skin, her cheeks the color of her pink dress.

"We're in apple country now," Gretel explained, waving her hand at the green fields dotted with heavily laden fruit trees, "one of New York state's major crops."

Laurie tore her eyes from the sleeping child to look out the window at the acres of trees, trying to pay attention to what Gretel was saying. *Young and foolish.* Laurie didn't ever want to be young and foolish again, not foolish enough to fall in love with a married pilot and foolish enough to believe him when he said he loved her.

Gretel continued her lecture on the cultivation of apples until they arrived at a cobblestone house set on a rise above the orchard. Laurie stood in the living room of the vintage structure admiring the rustic furniture, the Native American blankets hanging on the wall and the huge old fireplace while Gretel rushed to answer the ringing telephone in the kitchen.

When Gretel reappeared with Morgan in her arms, her expression was anxious and her face a shade paler than before. "That was Steve," she said. "He's finished his agriculture course early and wants me to come right away."

Laurie spread her arms out, palms up. "Well, why not? I'm here. You haven't seen him in what, six weeks? You haven't taken a vacation together since your honeymoon. I say go for it."

Laurie hugged her daughter to her and sat down on the couch. "You're right, I know you're right. It's just that—I've never even left Morgan overnight before. When you offered to stay with her I was—I *am* so grateful. But..." Gretel's lower lip trembled as she buried her face in her daughter's red curls.

Laurie watched the interplay between mother and daughter and her heart filled with sympathy and a touch of envy. If things had been different, if she'd been more sensible...

"It must sound silly to you," Gretel went on, "but you'll understand when you have a baby of your own."

One of her own. Laurie felt a lump form in her throat. With her luck she had small hope of having one of her own, let alone finding a man to have a baby with. She nodded at Gretel. "I understand perfectly."

"You're a true friend," Gretel said earnestly, "the best. Don't think I don't appreciate what you're offering, staying with a teething baby while I fly off to take a second honeymoon. If I weren't such a worry-wart— Come on," Gretel said, getting to her feet. "You must be tired. I'll show you your room. I told Steve I'd sleep on it and let him know tomorrow."

The guest room was furnished in the same style as the rest of the house, with a handmade quilt on the antique iron bed frame and a large oak armoire against the wall. After Gretel said good-night and took the baby with her down the hall, Laurie sat on the edge of the bed, her stocking feet resting on a handwoven braid rug, and tried to stifle the feelings of envy that threatened to engulf her. A charming old house, a husband and a baby. What more could anyone want?

She shook off her unbecoming feelings and got undressed. In bed, snuggled under a fluffy comforter, Laurie told herself now that she'd quit her job with the airline and forgotten about the handsome but *married* pilot who'd nearly broken her heart, she had her whole life ahead of her, that anything was possible, that all her dreams *could* come true. But the niggling questions remained: How, When, Where and Who?

The next day Gretel called Steve back and told him she couldn't leave so soon and she and Laurie and Morgan headed off to see the sights. Morgan was tucked safely in her car seat, gnawing happily on her teething ring. It was Gretel who didn't look happy. Not the next day nor the day after that. No matter how interesting the pictures in the art museum or how dazzling the view of Ontario from the Peace Bridge, she was racked with indecision about when to leave.

"So, Morgan," Laurie said one afternoon as she held the little girl in her lap and fed her applesauce. "Shall we put your mother on the next plane for Seattle before she has a chance to change her mind?" Each day Laurie found herself growing more attached to her goddaughter, and Morgan was more willing to go to Laurie when her mother was tired or busy.

Gretel gave Laurie a wry smile. "How did you know what I was thinking?" she asked.

"Intuition," Laurie answered. "I've known you a long time. Longer than Morgan here. And she and I agree that it's time for you to cut the cord. Vamoose, skeedaddle, be on your way."

Reluctantly Gretel met Laurie's gaze. "But we haven't seen the Falls yet. I've been saving it for last. And a friend of Steve's was going to give us a personal tour. A gorgeous guy. I wanted you to meet him."

"Morgan and I can see the Falls on our own. We don't need a guide, no matter how gorgeous, do we, Morgan? After we drop you at the airport, we'll go." Laurie put Morgan in her high chair and reached for the phone. "I'll make the reservation for you. You're ready. You've been packed for days."

Gretel listened to Laurie and watched her write down the flight information. She didn't say yes and she didn't say no. She did call Steve, though, and gave him her flight number. She didn't change her mind, but she came close. She hugged Morgan and said goodbye a dozen times. At the airport she walked down the long tunnel to the plane with one very wistful backward glance at Laurie and her daughter. Laurie smiled confidently and even Morgan waved to her mother before the plane took off.

Laurie turned to Morgan in her arms just as the baby screwed up her face into a frown and began to scream.

Chapter Two

Once in her car seat, Morgan turned bright red and flailed her arms in anger and frustration. It could have been her teeth, but Laurie suspected she was witnessing separation anxiety the likes of which she'd never imagined. And Gretel had barely left!

Laurie gripped the steering wheel tightly and wondered what to do. She realized, belatedly, that she didn't know anything about babies except that she wanted one. Would Morgan prefer to go home or would she rather see Niagara Falls the way her mother had planned before she took off? Morgan didn't say. She just cried as if her heart were broken.

So Laurie decided on the Falls. Maybe Morgan needed a distraction. Laurie certainly did. With one hand on the steering wheel, she reached into the glove compartment with the other for the map. Gretel had marked the route and Laurie soon saw the signs for the tollway.

Laurie kept driving and Morgan kept crying until they reached the parking lot for the viewing area of Niagara Falls. The noise of the white water was thunderous, almost loud enough to drown out Morgan's sobs. Laurie unbuckled the baby from her seat, shoved the car keys into her pocket and grabbed Morgan's backpack and diaper bag, all the while keeping up a line of chatter designed to soothe the child. With Morgan on her back and the diaper bag over her arm, Laurie approached the fence and gasped at the sight.

The water cascaded to a two-hundred foot drop sending a mist back up into the air. It was stunning. It was breathtaking. But not to Morgan. Her wailing reached new heights. Other tourists stopped snapping pictures of each other and looked at the baby. A man at the edge of the crowd stared at them. Probably wondering what torture Laurie was inflicting on the poor child.

"Please, Morgan," Laurie begged under her breath. "Please don't cry. Look at the Falls. Aren't they beautiful?"

Laurie sank down onto a wooden bench, lifted Morgan out of the backpack and onto her lap. And Morgan continued to cry. Desperate, Laurie reached into her pocket, pulled out her car keys and rattled them in front of Morgan.

The baby stopped crying instantly, grabbed the keys out of Laurie's hand and threw them over the fence and down into the depths of the turbulent Niagara River.

Laurie gasped, stood and looked with disbelief into the white water. "Morgan," she breathed, "what have you done?" A better question was, what had Laurie done, handing her keys to a baby to play with?

Cooper Buckingham asked himself the same question as he watched the improbable scene unfold from only ten feet away. Who could be so dumb as to give a baby her keys? What would she do now, he wondered, call her husband to come and get her? Thank God *he* wasn't married to a ditzy blonde like that. He wasn't married to anyone or he wouldn't be a consultant with a new job every few months—this one at the Niagara Power Project. Normally he didn't take time out to stand and stare at a woman with a baby, but that baby over there had started crying again now that the keys were gone.

What would the tall, slender blonde with the bright spots of color in her cheeks do next? He didn't wait to find out. He'd seen enough. Let the baby's father rescue them. He had problems of his own to worry about. Problems that involved water flow, hydropower, transmission lines, turbines and spin generators. And these problems almost always kept him too busy to contemplate the problems or pleasures a family might provide.

Just before he turned to leave, the woman looked in his direction, straight into Cooper's eyes, as if she'd read his thoughts, as if she knew exactly what he was thinking. The look she gave him might have also been a plea for help. If it weren't for the proud tilt of her chin, it would have been. But somehow he knew this woman wasn't used to asking for help.

And even if she asked, what could he do? He knew nothing about babies, or how to retrieve car keys from the bottom of the Falls, had no interest in blondes with the cool, devastatingly beautiful good looks with or without babies. Assuring himself that her husband would be along any minute, he shrugged, turned his back on her and headed toward the nearby hotel where he was staying.

Laurie staggered back to the parking lot with Morgan over one shoulder, clutching the diaper bag and the backpack in her hand. There she leaned against Gretel's Jeep, her knees threatening to buckle underneath her. But the longer she stayed there, so close to the car she couldn't drive, the more she felt like bursting into tears of her own.

It was Sunday afternoon and she was on the edge of Niagara Falls, surrounded by tourists, miles from the nearest Jeep dealer, with no way to get there. She looked at her watch. It was past Morgan's lunchtime. It was past her lunchtime, too. Maybe she'd think more clearly if she had something to eat. Maybe Morgan would stop crying if she had something to eat. Still dragging all the baby paraphernalia, she headed for the hotel on the other side of the road.

The waiter in the carpeted dining room showed them to a table by the window and brought a high chair for the baby. Laurie pulled a bottle of juice from Morgan's bag. The little girl gulped thirstily. "Is that what you wanted, sweetheart?" Laurie said hopefully. If only she weren't so worried, she could enjoy the spectacular view of white water and cliffs and boats in the river below, but her mind spun frantically even as she ordered a club sandwich and a sparkling water.

But before her sandwich arrived, Morgan put her juice down and wrinkled her face into a grimace. Laurie knew what was coming next. An earsplitting scream followed by loud wailing.

They couldn't stay in the dining room. She should have chosen the coffee shop, or better yet, a hole in the ground to hide. Now there was nowhere to go. Laurie bent over and reached for a handful of toys and a jar of baby food from the large, lined bag and frantically pried the lid open. But Morgan ignored her toys and the strained beets. Morgan's attention was somewhere else. And then suddenly she was waving her arms happily, cooing and gurgling at something or someone more interesting across the room.

Laurie turned to see what it was. There, not two tables away, sat the man from the parking lot. The man who'd given her a look that said more clearly than words that she was an idiot for giving the baby her car keys, that she never should have brought a crying, teething baby to the Falls in the first place. The look he'd given her contained not a shred of sympathy for her plight, just disapproval and disbelief.

Quickly she turned her back on him and gave her attention to the baby who was now playing peekaboo with the stranger from behind her chair. "Morgan," she whispered urgently, "stop that right away. Leave the man alone. He's not your type. Not mine, either," she added. She was through with good-looking men who didn't like children. She could spot them a mile away and she wasn't going to let her goddaughter fall for one the way she had.

"Look," she said, unwraping a cracker and showing it to Morgan. But Morgan wasn't interested. She was too busy flirting with the man. And what was he doing? Laurie didn't want to know. On the other hand, she felt an uncontrollable urge to take another look at him. Just to make sure she wasn't wrong about him.

No, she wasn't. He was looking at Morgan with a reluctant half smile on his ruggedly handsome face. But when he suddenly shifted his gaze toward Laurie she felt her pulse race uncontrollably. What was wrong with her? She, who'd been hit on by all kinds of men in all kinds of restaurants, bars and airplanes, was reacting to a glance from a stranger? She told herself to stay cool, told herself to ignore the tingling feeling traveling up and down her spine as their eyes met, broke apart and met again.

The nerve of the man. Making time with her goddaughter and now her, too. This was ridiculous. She forced herself to turn back to the table, deliberately picked up the wine list and studied it like a connoisseur, although she never drank during the day. Her cheeks were hot and her skin was shivery. She had the distinct feeling the man was still looking at her and that he'd left his table and was walking toward them.

When she tore her eyes from the leather-bound list of wines, she saw she was right. The man was standing behind the vacant place at their table, his broad fingers spread across the back of the empty chair. He reached into his pocket and held up a small plastic troll with blue hair. "Is this yours?" he asked.

Laurie's already flaming cheeks turned even redder. "Thank you," she said, holding out her hand.

"I found it in the lobby," he said, handing it to Morgan.

Embarrassed, Laurie drew her hand back. Meeting the man's gaze up close was different from meeting it across the viewing area or even from two tables away. His eyes were a deep blue and flashed with enough energy to make her toes curl inside her walking shoes.

"Maybe you dropped it," he said, sliding into the vacant chair at their table.

Laurie opened her mouth to answer when she saw he was talking to Morgan. She was getting irritated at being left out of this conversation. "Or maybe it fell out of the bag," she said. "In any case, we're grateful to you." *So now you can go,* she thought.

"I thought it was hers," he said, unaware of her hostility. "I noticed her in the parking lot."

"She noticed you, too," Laurie admitted. She didn't admit she'd done her share of noticing, too. "I think you remind her of someone." He reminded Laurie of someone, too, someone she'd rather forget.

"Her father?" he asked.

Laurie let her gaze drift from the dark hair that slanted across his forehead to the strong jaw and the broad shoulders. She shook her head. "No, not her father." Morgan's father was stocky with red hair.

"Too bad he can't be here," he remarked, reaching for the crackers Morgan had thrown on the floor, and handing them back to her.

"Yes, well..." Laurie folded and refolded her napkin in her lap as the waiter delivered her sandwich along with a bottle of imported beer to the man. "He's already seen it, I mean them." She waved her hand in the direction of the magnificent display of falling water outside the window. There was a long moment of silence while they all stared out the window. Even Morgan seemed impressed by the fifty thousand cubic feet of water per second that flowed over the precipice.

When the waiter returned to bring him his turkey sandwich, Coop paused and considered taking the sandwich and moving back to his table. He couldn't even remember why he'd left in the first place. Oh, yes, the toy. It certainly wasn't to admire the baby, though he had to admit it was flattering to think he could make her stop crying. And it certainly wasn't to pick up some married woman. He had no intention of picking up any woman at all. Then why was he here, retrieving falling objects for a baby and coming on to a beautiful blonde who didn't say she was and didn't say she wasn't married?

Curiosity, he told himself. Pure and simple. The same scientific curiosity that led him to the field of hydraulic engineering. To find out how to recover the maximum amount of energy from a river without destroying its natural beauty. His eyes strayed to the curve of Laurie's cheek, the straight line of her nose, the indentation of her throat. Speaking of natural beauty...

"I'm Cooper Buckingham. I work here at the dam. Mind if I join you?" he heard himself say as if he hadn't already joined them. "Or are you waiting for someone?"

After a brief pause she shook her head. "We're alone for now. I'm Laurie Clayton and this is Morgan."

"What's wrong with Morgan?" he asked, reaching for the troll that Morgan had thrown to the floor a few minutes ago.

Laurie sighed and looked from him to the baby. "Nothing as long as you're around. I don't know how you do it. She stopped crying when she saw you. You have a real knack with children. I suppose you have several at home?" Laurie dipped into the strained beets with a small spoon in a gallant attempt to feed them to Morgan. But Morgan swerved her head at the last minute and the beets sprayed onto her little blue outfit.

Coop watched the scene unfold, dismayed by the mess, but even more so by the question she asked. Why on earth had he joined these two and why did she have to pry into his life? "No kids," he answered brusquely. "No wife, either. I travel light, work on temporary assignments like this one. Here for a few months, then on to the next place. Which reminds me—" he signaled the waiter "—I've got to get back to work."

Laurie nodded and reached for her purse. But all she came up with was the diaper bag. A cold chill came over her despite the wool sweater she had over her shoulders. Frantically she looked around the chair, on the floor and in the diaper bag. She couldn't, she didn't, she wouldn't have left her purse in the locked car, would she? Oh, no, no, no... Cooper was holding the check, her check? His check? *Their* check and stared at her horrified expression.

"I...uh...seem to have left my purse in the car," she confessed.

"And the car's locked?" he asked.

"Yes," she admitted, "and Morgan threw the keys into the Falls."

He nodded. "I saw that." He took his credit card from his wallet and laid it on the table. "This is on me, then."

"I can't let you do that," she protested. "Give me your address so I can send you the money."

"Don't worry about it. It's taken care of. What about your car?"

Laurie's face flushed. She hoped he didn't think she did this on purpose. "The car? Oh, yes, the car. I'm just going to call a friend to come and get it and me...and Morgan."

"Not your husband?" he inquired with a raised eyebrow.

"No, not my husband. I don't have a husband."

"Just a baby," he suggested.

"Not a baby, either. Morgan isn't mine. She's my goddaughter. I'm just babysitting. That's why I don't know what to do when she cries or throws things. But I'm learning." She gave Cooper what she hoped was a confident smile. Then she picked up the bag, the backpack and extricated Morgan from the high chair and after another smile and more thanks she strode out of the dining room with what she imagined was great dignity. Which was marred only by the sound of Morgan, who, upon realizing they were leaving Cooper, began to cry all over again.

"Morgan," she murmured, heading for the public telephone in the lobby of the hotel, but having no idea who to call. "Don't cry like that. Not over a man. They aren't worth it. I know. Especially that kind. The kind who travels light. Who isn't married and doesn't want to be. Who has no children and doesn't want any. Believe me, I know."

Plunking her equipment on the floor and lifting Morgan up onto her shoulder, Laurie stared at the telephone, then picked up a brochure for the hotel that boasted rooms with no TV or radio, just wall-to-wall views of the Falls and the river, overstuffed chairs, old-fashioned tubs and extra large beds with down quilts.

Laurie looked longingly at the glossy photographs, picturing herself sinking into the depths of a down quilt. An odor permeated her thoughts and Laurie wrinkled her nose. She suddenly realized that Morgan needed a new diaper. Now. She had to do something, find enough space to change her, then give her a nap. Then she had to find a way to get home. If she had money she'd call a cab. But she didn't.

First things first. The diaper. The ladies' room. But Morgan didn't want to go to the ladies' room. She cried louder and louder. Laurie couldn't move, couldn't think.

* * *

From the lobby where he was meeting with three other engineers, Cooper heard the frantic cries. How could he miss them? He could have suggested another meeting place like the bar. But he didn't. He excused himself and walked in the direction of the loud crying and found them by the telephones.

"What's wrong?" he asked, as if he didn't know.

At the mere sound of his voice, Morgan stopped crying, squirmed in Laurie's arms and looked at Cooper through tear-soaked eyelashes. Then she held out her arms to him, a man she'd never seen before that day, a man she knew nothing about except that her godmother told her to beware of him. But he did nothing, this man she adored. He just stood there, his gaze shifting back and forth between the two of them, his arms at his sides, waiting for her answer.

"Nothing," Laurie said at last. "Nothing at all. My car keys are at the bottom of the Niagara River, my purse is locked inside the car, the baby desperately needs a new diaper and I have no way to get home."

"Other than that, is everything okay?" he asked with a faint smile.

"Just great," she assured him as Morgan leaned toward him, making little baby sounds that were hard to ignore. But Cooper did. He continued to stand with his arms locked at his sides, his forehead creased, an uncertain look in his dark blue eyes. Then, without Coop knowing quite how it happened, perhaps through sheer willpower, Morgan transferred herself from her godmother to him. She threw her chubby arms around his neck while he awkwardly put his hands around her wet, diapered bottom.

He'd never held a baby in his arms before. Wet or dry. He would have remembered if he had. The feeling was unforgettable. She was heavier than a sack of flour, and harder to get a hold on even with her arms wrapped around his neck in a death grip. When she pressed her tearstained cheek against his, he looked over her head at Laurie, who was watching him with wide brown eyes, an anxious expression on her face.

His own feelings were pretty anxious at that point. There was a tightness in his chest, a shortness of breath he couldn't explain except to think it was sheer terror. He wanted to give the baby back, but he didn't want her to start that horrible crying again. He wanted to go back to the lobby, to continue his meeting, but he couldn't do that, either, not when they had no way home. What happened to "the friend," he wondered. Maybe there was no friend. No friend and no husband. Just one beautiful, if inept substitute mother and one wet baby. He held Morgan out and Laurie took her back.

"You can change her in my room," he said reluctantly. He wanted to say, "but that's all." But he didn't.

"You're staying here?" she asked, patting the baby gently on the back.

"It's convenient. Close to work and the food in the dining room's decent. I'm not here long enough to rent a house."

"Well, if you don't mind," she said. "Then we'll get out of your way."

He didn't ask how they'd get out of his way. He was afraid to. Wasn't it enough he'd made the baby stop crying and was now offering his room as a changing area? They *wouldn't,* they *couldn't* ask him for a ride home, too, could they?

They didn't ask anything. No one spoke at all in the elevator to the third floor. While Cooper phoned the lobby and made excuses to his colleagues, Laurie quickly and efficiently changed Morgan's diaper in the commodious tiled bathroom that smelled faintly of sandlewood soap and after-shave. Returning to the bedroom with a dry, clean, quiet Morgan, Laurie looked around. With a fire laid in the fireplace, the room looked just as inviting as the pictures in the brochure.

"Put her on the bed for a minute," Cooper said. "You look like you could use a rest."

Laurie knew how she looked. She'd caught a glimpse of herself in the mirror over the sink. Tangled hair, smudged face, shirt streaked with purple beets. But it was more important to clean up Morgan than herself. She'd do it later when she got home.... Oh God, she'd almost forgotten. She had no way to get home. But she spread a baby blanket in the middle of the king-size bed and put Morgan down on her stomach. Just for a minute. Just until she caught her breath. Until she decided what to do.

Then she sat on the edge of the bed watching the baby's eyelids flutter closed. "I never knew they could wear you out like that," she mused. "What do people do who have more than one?"

"They don't give them their car keys to play with," Coop observed dryly from the easy chair at the window where he'd stretched his long legs out in front of him.

Laurie bit her lower lip to keep it from trembling. She didn't need to have her stupidity pointed out to her.

"How about a drink?" he asked, crossing the room and unlocking the small, well-stocked refrigerator. "You look like you need one."

"I *know* what I look like," she said, dabbing at a spot on the front of her shirt. "You don't have to remind me." For one moment she thought longingly of her old life handing out trays and filling drink orders in an impeccable uniform with every hair in place. But a glance at Morgan's flushed cheeks, her little clenched fists made her smile in spite of her weariness.

Ignoring her remark, Coop poured her a glass of chilled white wine. What she didn't seem to know was that her tangled blond hair and wrinkled clothes only accentuated her classic features. She wasn't vain. That was rare in a woman with her looks. Cooper knew that much.

"I really shouldn't," she said, taking the wine from him. "I've got to stay focused and try to decide how to get out of this mess."

His hand brushed hers and she looked up, startled at the rush of adrenaline that pulsed through her body. His eyes met hers just for a second, then he touched his glass to hers. "Here's to your safe return," he said and sat down next to her on the bed. She took a sip of wine, wondering if he had to sit so close on such a large bed, so close his leg was pressed against hers. She became aware of the muscles in his thigh, the heat from his body, the beating of his heart. Or was that *her* heart? Suddenly she had to hold her glass with two hands to keep it steady.

"The way I see it," he said, his face so close she could see his eyes were really a deep navy, and his hair looked so soft and thick she had an uncontrollable desire to run her hands through it, "you have two choices."

"What are they?" she asked breathlessly. She was unable to move in any direction, to even look away from the stranger who'd paid for her lunch, invited her to his hotel room and was now plying her with white wine and coming closer with every passing second. Where was Morgan when Laurie needed a chaperon? Conked out on the bed. On the *other* side of the bed.

Coop paused. He was stalling for time. He didn't know what to say. The only choices that came to mind had nothing to do with car keys or a sleeping baby. They had to do with the woman next to him. The same woman he wanted nothing to do with. He still didn't. He just . . . couldn't seem to get away from her. There was something about the way she was handling this crisis, the loss of her keys, the cranky baby, that summoned his grudging admiration. It was partly the way she picked up the baby and walked out of the restaurant, as if she hadn't a care in the world, that made him want to help her.

Under her bravado was a vulnerability he couldn't seem to ignore. But he had to ignore her. He couldn't do any more for her. Except maybe call a cab. While he thought about it, he wondered if her hair felt the way it looked, like pale silk. And what made her smell like hothouse flowers, her lotion or her perfume? Was that desire that flared in her eyes a minute ago, or just a reflection of what he felt? He wasn't going to hang around and find out. Not now. Not ever.

He didn't know anything about this woman, not really. Only that she said the baby wasn't hers. That she'd lost her keys *and* her credit card was locked in the car. It was possible. Anything was possible. Anything but taking her home himself. Two choices, he'd said. And one was . . .

"I could take you home," he heard himself say. Now where did *that* come from?

Chapter Three

With Laurie sitting next to him, the baby in the back seat, Cooper began the long drive toward the truck farming region outside of Buffalo. They drove in silence. Only occasionally did he glance in her direction, each time silently admiring her profile in the twilight, the honey gold hair that brushed her cheek.

Finally she spoke. "I really appreciate this," she said. "I don't know what I would have done without you today. I guess I'd still be in the hotel lobby."

"Wouldn't Morgan's parents eventually come and get you?" he asked.

"They're out of town, both of them. That's why I'm here. Gretel, that's Morgan's mother, is my best friend. We used to fly together for Northeast Air. Then Gretel got married and moved to this apple orchard."

Cooper turned to look at her. "This story sounds familiar."

"I suppose it is. Woman has fun job. Meets man of her dreams. Quits job, lives happily ever after in apple orchard."

"No, I mean it sounds *really* familiar," he said. "Like something that happened to a friend of mine."

"You have a friend who worked for the airline, too?"

"I have a friend who married a flight attendant and who lives on an apple orchard around here. Name's Steve Lundgren."

Laurie's mouth fell open. "You're kidding. That's Gretel's husband."

"What a coincidence. We were supposed to get together, but he's been taking an agricultural course in Washington. I offered to give his wife, Gretel, a tour of the Falls, but she never called me. Anyway..." His voice trailed off. He'd avoided calling them, the way he'd been avoiding other old friends who might look at him with pity in their eyes, who might even try to fix him up with unmarried friends like Laurie here. Just what he didn't want. Just what he didn't need.

"It's a small world," Laurie murmured. Gretel's words came back to her. *A gorgeous guy. I wanted you to meet him.* Well, she'd met him. And he was gorgeous, but he took her for a dimwit, a woman who couldn't manage a day on her own without losing her keys, her purse and her self-esteem. And he'd be likely to pass on his opinion to Steve and Gretel as soon as he saw them. "How do you know Steve?" she asked, trying to fill the empty silence.

"We went to school together," he said. "Fraternity brothers actually."

"I suppose you'll have a lot of catching up to do when you see him. How long has it been?"

He shrugged as if he couldn't remember. But he remembered. Two years ago. At the funeral. "I really don't know his wife," he said, quickly changing the subject. "You say she quit her job?"

"When Morgan was born. She still has her benefits, so that's how she was able to join Steve and take a second honeymoon. She just left today. That's why Morgan's so upset." Laurie looked in the rearview mirror to see that the child was fast asleep.

"*Was* upset," she continued, "until you came along. Anyway that's why we're alone, just the two of us." Laurie took a breath. She couldn't seem to stop talking, now that she'd started. You'd think Gretel had been gone for days instead of hours, she was so desperate to talk to an adult. "We were planning to go to the Falls before Gretel left, so I decided to come anyway. Now I wish I'd never seen that spectacular sight."

Cooper didn't answer, so Laurie continued. "I guess you wish you'd never seen *us*. Then you'd be watching the Falls illuminated at night from the comfort of your hotel room instead of transporting two helpless females across the state."

"I've seen the Falls at night," he remarked, "and I'll see them again. How far did you say it was?"

She bit her lip, hearing an underlying impatience in his voice. "I'm not exactly sure, but I know it's the River Road Exit we want." She couldn't believe she'd thrown herself at the mercy of this man. But what choice did she have? This was no time for pride. She had Morgan to think of. "You probably won't believe this," she said, "but Morgan is normally a wonderful baby, except when she's teething or her mother leaves, and then—" Laurie sighed. "Well, you saw what happened. I feel so helpless. I wish I had your knack with children. How do you do it?"

"I don't. It's never happened before. In my line of work I rarely run into babies or many women for that matter. Believe me, I'm not out looking for them," he said emphatically.

Laurie didn't say anything. What could she say when a man made it perfectly clear he wanted nothing to do with her or Morgan? But even if Cooper Buckingham wasn't out looking for women, he had to have them falling all over him with that animal magnetism he radiated and those devastating good looks. Why hadn't Gretel said more about him? Why hadn't Laurie asked?

Cooper hoped Laurie had gotten the message. He didn't want to talk about women and babies. He'd successfully turned his attention to his work these past years, locking his past into a tiny compartment deep inside. Any threat to his hard-won peace of mind had to be vigorously avoided. Not that this chance encounter was a threat. Within an hour these two would be out of his car and out of his life. If Steve or Gretel called him when they got back and tried to arrange something, he'd say he was busy. It usually worked with everyone else. There was no reason to worry, no cause to panic. It was time to change the subject from him to her.

"Do you still work for the airline?" he asked.

"I quit a few months ago. I got tired of the rat race, so I...I..." She turned her face to the window and pressed her forehead against it.

Puzzled, he looked at her slender shoulders, which were shaking, and her blond straight hair that brushed against her sweater. "What's wrong? What did I say?" he asked.

"Nothing," she answered in a muffled voice.

Startled, he asked, "Are you crying?"

She shook her head. "Of course not. I just...can't talk about it yet. I haven't even told Gretel."

"Told her what?"

"Why I quit."

"Why *did* you quit?" The woman was baffling, maddening. What *was* her problem? Schizophrenia? Agoraphobia? Vertigo?

"It's so stupid, you won't believe it."

"Try me," he suggested.

"I fell in love with a pilot," she confessed in a ragged voice.

"So?"

"He was married."

"Oh."

His tone said it all. He'd lost all respect for her. If he had any to begin with. "I knew it. It was my fault. He said he was getting a divorce. He said it was almost final. It wasn't." She took a deep breath, wondering what had loosened her tongue—the wine in his room, the company or the long ride. "That was six months ago. I should be over it by now. I *am* over it.

It's finished and I'm fine. I don't know why I'm telling you all this. I don't even know you.''

Suddenly she felt his hand close over hers on the car seat. Sympathy from a total stranger, just what she didn't want. And yet, the warmth of his hand stole through her body, infusing her with a heat that flooded her veins. Blinking back tears, she turned to face him in the darkness of the car.

''Sometimes it's easier to talk to a stranger,'' he said.

She nodded. ''That must be it. I feel much better. Thanks. Again. Oh, there's the sign. It can't be too far now. She pulled her hand away self-consciously and straightened her shoulders. She was glad he couldn't see her face, glad she couldn't see his. See his expression of pity, and know what he thought of her. Equally glad she'd probably never see him again after today.

In another half hour they were driving up the road to the farmhouse. Cooper followed her into the house, all the way into Morgan's room, and he watched while she laid the baby carefully, without waking her, into her crib.

Coop stood there watching Morgan sigh contentedly, snuggle into her blanket, the night-light shining on her rosy skin, and suddenly felt a tightening in his chest, a poignant longing for something he'd lost and could never find again. The feelings that this baby awakened, that this woman caused made his heart rate accelerate. What was it? Fear of involvement? Certainly not *desire* for involvement. He felt Laurie's eyes on him and he reached for her hand for the second time that evening. This time she gripped his fingers and didn't let go.

The curtains fluttered in the breeze and the sweet scent of ripening apples floated in through the window. He turned slightly to meet her gaze and desire shot through him, as sudden as it was unwanted. He hardly knew this woman, and yet he did know her somehow. He wanted her, wanted to cup her head with his hands and kiss her deeply, profoundly. But he wouldn't have touched her if she hadn't moved her hands up his arms and gripped his shoulders.

"Cooper," she whispered, her voice tinged with surprise, and his heart thudded in his chest. The smell of the ripe fruit outside mingled with her scent and became one. She moved closer to him, her face tilted toward his, her lips parted, inviting. Did she know what she was doing? Did she know what she wanted? Did she feel a fraction of the desire that swept through him?

He pulled her to him until her breasts were crushed against his chest. She gasped but she didn't back away. Her eyes were filled with questions he couldn't answer. There were no answers, he realized with a sudden shock. It was wrong to think there were. He dropped his arms and she took a step backward, blinking uncomprehendingly. Then the phone in the other room began to ring and she turned on her heel and walked out the door.

When he steadied himself and joined her in the living room she was talking on the phone.

"It was all my fault," she explained.

Not exactly, he thought. In fact, he was to blame for what happened. For letting her think this could be the start of something.

"I'll get a new set of keys tomorrow in Buffalo.... Yes, I know. And Morgan's been a real trouper through it all. A perfect angel." Her gaze met Cooper's across the room and she gave him a half smile. He heard her ask about the weather in Seattle and how Steve was. The only clue that she'd been wrapped in his arms a few minutes ago was a telltale flush that clung to her cheekbones.

He didn't want to stand there and listen to her talk. He wanted to take the phone out of her hands and take up where they'd left off. He wanted to toss her sweater across the floor, unbutton her shirt, capture her breasts in his hands, watch her eyes darken with desire, hear her whisper his name again—but that was not going to happen.

He stood and walked to the window to let the night air cool his face. What was it about her that turned him into a maniac? He was not in the market for a short-term relationship, or a long-term one, either. His only goal was to avoid pain. Cooper had suffered enough pain to last a lifetime. He had to ignore this overwhelming attraction, and the electricity that crackled in the air whenever she was around.

She hung up at last and he turned to face her, but the phone rang again. He pounded his fist into his palm with frustration. He had to say goodbye and get out of there. She talked for a few minutes, then hung up again.

"My sister," Laurie explained. Her sister who wanted to know if she'd met anyone interesting yet. Her sister who wouldn't rest until Laurie found as much love and happiness as she had. Who didn't realize yet that taking care of a baby was a full-time job, with no time left over to look for interesting men. Unless they just happened to be in the right place at the wrong time.

"You must be starving," she said, pressing her palms against her heated cheeks. "I am. Let's see what Gretel left us. I know there're apples, pounds and pounds of apples." She was chattering, trying to cover up her nervousness while Cooper remained silent, just watching her. She still tasted his lips on hers, still felt his hands pulling her close, then closer. She still wanted more, but knew she couldn't have it, not here, not now, not with him.

This man wasn't interested in what she was interested in. She was not about to fall for somebody else who couldn't or wouldn't get married. The next time she fell in love it would be with someone who was looking for a home and a hearth and a baby. And a wife, of course. This man wasn't. She didn't know why and she didn't care. It was none of her business.

Nonetheless she owed him something for bringing her and Morgan all the way home tonight. Dinner. She opened the refrigerator and stared at the contents without seeing them. With Coop standing next to her, hair rumpled, eyes gleaming dangerously, she had a hard time focusing on food.

"Can you cook?" he asked.

"Not really," she confessed. "But I'm good at heating things up."

His mouth quirked up at one corner and his eyes sparkled with interest. She felt her face flame despite the cool, refrigerated air. "I mean . . ."

"I know what you mean and I agree completely." He reached across her and pulled out a package of ground meat. "How about hamburgers?"

Laurie nodded gratefully, found buns in the freezer, lettuce in the crisper and very soon they were sitting at the breakfast nook in the kitchen eating salad and slathering mustard and ketchup on their burgers.

"This is great," she said between bites. "Too bad you're not in the marriage market. You could make some lucky woman very happy."

He filled her glass from a can of soda he found in the refrigerator. "By cooking hamburgers every night? I doubt it."

Laurie wiggled her toes happily, happy to be home, happy to be across the table from this good-looking but unavailable man who must be aware that cooking hamburgers was most definitely *not* all he could do. She swallowed a smile and a gulp of orange soda and said, "Sounds good to me."

"You must be desperate," he said jokingly. But the look in her eyes told him she wasn't amused. She was hurt. The look lasted only for a second, then she recovered with a quick smile that never quite reached her eyes. "I mean for good food," he explained.

She nodded and finished her sandwich.

He leaned back in Gretel's ladder-back kitchen chair. "You'll need a ride in to Buffalo tomorrow."

She got up from the table and carried the empty dishes to the dishwasher. "I can't ask you to do that."

"You don't have much of a choice," he remarked.

She leaned against the counter and looked at him. No, she didn't have much of a choice. But the ramifications had her mind spinning. If he drove her in he'd have to spend the night and that worried her. Not that he was going to take advantage of her. If anyone was taking advantage of anyone, she was the guilty party. Who was it who threw herself at him in the nursery tonight? Who couldn't carry on a coherent phone conversation with him in the same room? If she could only control herself for one night, she didn't need to worry about him. After all, he was a friend of the family. And Morgan liked him. Didn't babies have inherent good intuition?

She took a deep breath. "It's nice of you to offer, but really—you could, I mean if you really don't mind, well, there's the spare bedroom, the one I was in. I'll move into Gretel's—" She was chattering again, and making no sense, hoping he wouldn't get the wrong idea, that she *wanted* him to stay, when what she really wanted was...what was it again?

He nodded and stretched his arms over his head as if it was fine with him, whatever she arranged. It was Laurie who couldn't stop thinking of him sleeping in her bed in the guest room, with his long legs tangled in the sheets she'd slept in. It was Laurie who couldn't take her eyes off his arms as he stretched, watching the muscles flex, measuring the width of his shoulders, noticing the way his hair fell across his forehead, almost daring her to smooth it back from his face.

"If you're sure you can spare the time, that is," she continued, not knowing if it was settled or not. "If you don't really have to go to work..."

He shook his head and stood up from the table. "As a consultant, I can pretty much set my own hours. And this job is about finished anyway. It's the least I can do for Gretel and Steve. It's not like I'm a total stranger. At least you know I'm not likely to get up in the night and steal the silverware."

Laurie knew it was risky. Not that he'd steal the silverware, but that he'd steal her heart. Her vulnerable heart. But that wasn't going to happen. Not to the new Laurie. The new, stronger, wiser Laurie, who anticipated danger before it struck. Who could spot a love 'em and leave 'em man a mile away. And one who was as up-front about his intentions or lack of them as Cooper? No problem.

"Even if you weren't a friend of the family, I wouldn't worry about the silverware. After all, what would you do with it, if all you can cook is hamburgers? Besides, after all those years in the friendly skies, I can read people pretty well. And I know you aren't the sneaky type."

"Really?" He braced his hands against the kitchen counter and slanted a provocative glance at her. "What type am I?"

There was something about the look in his blue eyes that sucked the breath right out of her lungs. That challenged her to say he was *her* type, when she knew he wasn't. As if she hadn't been hit on by every sexy, flirtatious passenger there ever was. But this was different. No man had ever had this effect on her before. She shut her eyes for a minute to pull herself together. To think of an answer. What type was he?

"I'm not sure," she said weakly. "Would you like to see the guest room?" They passed Morgan's room as they walked down the hall single file. "I hope she doesn't wake you in the night."

"Nothing wakes me," he assured her.

After explaining how to close the shutters on the windows, Laurie slipped away down the hall without saying good-night. Who could blame her for wanting to avoid another scene. For all he knew she hadn't gotten the message. But she had. She really had. Loud and clear. This man is not interested.

Cooper stripped down to his underwear and got between the sheets. They smelled of Laurie's flower scent that clung to her hair and her skin. He pressed his face into the pillow and inhaled deeply. Good God, what was wrong with him?

He'd led a celibate life for the past two years, neither looking for nor wanting anything else. The only thing he wanted was his wife and baby back. But that wasn't possible. In one night—one tragic night—everything he loved had been taken away from him. It was all he could do to keep it in the past, to keep it from intruding on his everyday life. He struggled with it, suffered through it and learned from it. What he learned was that no amount of happiness was worth the pain when it was gone. He would never ever take another chance on love again.

Yes, Laurie was an attractive woman. Morgan was an adorable baby—when she wasn't crying. But there was no reason for this chance encounter to leave him feeling restless, disturbed and filled with desires he thought were long buried.

He'd been on his way out the door when the next thing he knew he was cooking dinner for her. There was no need. Just because she couldn't cook didn't mean she would starve. All he needed to do was to say goodbye. And walk out. He certainly didn't need to drive her to Buffalo tomorrow. There were cabs. There were neighbors. But there was that look in her eyes, the look she tried to cover up when he'd made that remark about being desperate. He hadn't meant anything by it, but it had hurt her and he hadn't meant to.

He sighed loudly in the darkness. So she'd been hurt. She'd get over it. She *was* over it. She said so herself. But the look in her eyes said she wasn't quite over it. So he felt sorry for her. But that wasn't all.

It was also the novelty, he thought. After two years without a break, without a vacation, he was taking a day off. It was understandable that he'd feel off-balance. One more day with this woman and he'd be more than ready to go back to work, to the turbines, the water flow, the dynamos and the switchyards. He looked forward to it. Work was his solace. He liked troubleshooting. It kept his mind off himself and the past. It wasn't quite true what he'd said about the job being finished. There was always something he could do. But not tomorrow. Because tomorrow Laurie needed him.

He thought about the pilot with whom she'd fallen in love. Was she still in love with him? She'd get over it in time. She was tough, he knew that much about her, and she was beautiful, that was obvious. So beautiful she wouldn't be single for long as soon as she got back into circulation. As soon as she got out of this apple orchard and back into the real world. The thought of her surrounded by eligible men bothered him and kept him from sleeping. Or was it the sweet-smelling sheets that kept reminding him of the woman who'd last slept between them?

Chapter Four

"Did you know," Coop asked Laurie as they drove through Buffalo in a rainstorm the next day, "that this is one of the world's largest inland ports?"

"Is that why we keep driving by it?" Laurie asked, unfolding her map of the city for the third time.

"I keep driving by the port because I don't know where else to drive. You've got the map. Help me out here."

"I'm sorry," she said, spreading the map out in her lap. "I'm lost." Lost in the rain. The longer they drove around aimlessly the guiltier she felt. For taking up Cooper's day, for wasting his time, for interrupting his work. And now, besides thinking she was totally incompetent, he knew she couldn't read a map to save her soul. "Wait a minute," she said, "that was it, Main Street. Turn left . . . oh, too late."

His lips clamped together in an expression of disgust, Coop went around the block and got onto Main Street. Despite her guilt, despite the cold autumn rain, despite the annoyed expression on her companion's face, Laurie felt a strange sense of well-being. It might have been relief at finding the right street, or knowing they were on their way to getting her a new key to the Jeep. Or it might have been the cozy feeling of being sealed inside the car with Cooper and Morgan, the rain streaking down outside, creating their own little world inside.

And suddenly there it was, the Jeep dealer with its showroom full of shiny new Jeeps and an eager salesman rushing out to greet them.

"Perfect vehicle for the whole family," the salesman assured them, looking at Laurie who was holding Morgan.

"No, we really don't—"

"Something larger, more comfortable?"

"I don't think so, you see we're just—"

"Just looking," the salesman said with a knowing wink. "Go right ahead."

Laurie exchanged a helpless look with Cooper before they made their way to the service desk where they promptly obtained a new key for their vehicle.

"We don't look like a family, do we?" Cooper asked Laurie on their way back to the Falls under clearing skies.

"Of course not," she assured him, stealing a glance at his profile to admire his firm jaw, his jutting lower lip. "That's just what salesmen say. We look like . . . like a woman with her friend's baby and the man who took pity on them when she messed things up."

He gave her a half smile. "That's really what we look like?"

She nodded, wishing she could capture that rare smile, so she could remember it after he'd left, but it was gone in an instant. When they pulled up next to the Jeep in the parking lot at Niagara Falls, Laurie buckled Morgan back into her car seat and then stood for a moment, uncertain of what to say. Thank you was getting pretty old.

"Thanks again," she said at last.

He gave her a long look without saying anything and she wondered if he'd suggest seeing her again. But instead he took her by the shoulders and kissed her on the cheek. The kiss had goodbye written all over it.

"Bye," she said, swallowing the lump in her throat. Good grief, even after all they'd been through together, she hardly knew this man. Why shouldn't he say goodbye with a kiss, and why should she be upset if he did? It was just that she felt so grateful, so indebted, and now she wouldn't have a chance to repay him for all he'd done for her. That's what was bothering her. Sure it was.

"Will you be all right?" he asked, stepping back to look at her.

"Of course we will. But what about you? I hope you don't get into trouble for not coming to work today."

"I won't. Thanks for your hospitality." And then he was gone, walking briskly through the parking lot toward the hotel. Not a word about keeping in touch, or ever seeing her again. Not even a mention of Morgan who clearly adored him. Nothing about give my regards to Steve when you see him. No, he was clearly eager to get away. As soon as possible.

She started the Jeep with the new key and drove slowly back to the farm when Morgan began to cry. "Don't you start," Laurie warned over her shoulder, "or we'll both be crying. I told you he's not interested in us. You'll just have to accept that." But how could she expect Morgan to accept it if Laurie couldn't?

Coop stopped at the hotel only long enough to shower and change clothes, then he went to the power station where he stared at the giant turbines thinking there was no point in seeing Laurie again. Because it wouldn't work, not even as a short-term fling, not as anything. Yes, she was an irresistible combination of cool, blond good looks on the surface and passion underneath, but he'd vowed never to take a chance again. It wasn't worth it. No amount of pleasure was worth the pain he'd endured.

The best thing he could do right now was to bury himself in his work and forget her. He had to stop pretending he had only been doing her a favor by taking her in and driving her around when the truth was he couldn't seem to say goodbye. Even today, he'd kissed her farewell instead of saying it. How long would it take to forget her eyes, the color of autumn leaves and the petal softness of her skin? A few days maybe, but that was all. That's all the time he'd need.

But when she called him three days later, his heart did a half gainer in his chest at just the sound of her voice. She sounded hesitant and he could hear Morgan crying in the background. The sound he hated most.

"I hate to bother you," she began, "but I don't know who else to call."

"What's wrong?"

"It's the apples."

He heaved a sigh of relief. No lost keys, no rescue mission. "The apples? What's wrong with the apples?"

"They're ripe ahead of schedule. Gretel and Steve are still in Washington. I don't want to spoil their vacation, but there aren't enough workers to get the apples off the trees in time and I'm just not sure what I should do." She ran out of breath. "Am I overreacting?" she asked herself as well as Cooper.

"I don't know," he admitted. "What do you want me to do?"

"There's nothing you can do. I'm sorry to bother you, but I had to tell someone."

"What do you mean there's nothing I can do? I can pick apples."

"You can?"

"Anybody can pick apples."

"But you have a job."

"It's almost over. There's not that much to do except wrap things up."

She sucked in her breath. "I don't know what to say."

Cooper didn't hesitate. He didn't dare examine his motives for offering to help. All he knew was nothing could stop him from going back to the orchard. They might miss his presence at the power plant, but they didn't need him. Laurie needed him. It was as simple as that. Sure it was. "I'm on my way," he said. And he was.

After checking on Morgan who was napping peacefully, Laurie changed into an old pair of jeans she found in Gretel's closet and a ragged sweatshirt and pulled her hair into a ponytail.

She was in the orchard when Cooper found her, on top of a ladder she'd propped against the tree, repeating to herself what Gretel's farm hand had said. "The apple should break at the weakened point where the stem joins the fruiting spear," she muttered.

"What was that?" he asked, startling her so much she almost fell off the ladder. "I'm trying not to tear off next year's crop by pulling off the leaves and the fruiting spear, whatever that is." She held an apple in her hand and stared at it intently, so she wouldn't have to look down at his face and into his eyes. Just the sound of his voice was enough to set her legs shaking and she didn't want to start this venture by falling into his arms.

She shifted her weight carefully and braced herself against the tree trunk. Say something, she told herself. Say thanks for coming. Say you're glad to see him, even if glad isn't quite the word. She looked down into his eyes at last and her heart banged against her ribs. He was better looking than she remembered. Wearing old jeans and a flannel shirt with holes in the elbows, his hair a little longer, his eyes a little bluer, he looked as if he was ready for work. But she still wasn't sure why he was here. She kept telling herself his willingness had nothing to do with her.

"Thanks for coming," she said breathlessly, as if she'd just climbed a mountain instead of an apple tree. "You must think I can't do anything by myself."

"You can't pick an entire orchard by yourself," he said, glancing around the acres of ripe fruit trees. "No one can."

"The staff is here," she said, "the people who work year-round, spraying and pruning, so we're not alone. But we'll never get all the apples off the trees until the seasonal workers get here, and they're busy elsewhere. Darn this unusual weather."

"We can only try."

"You don't have to try. It's not your responsibility."

"Maybe not but I have an obligation to Steve. He'd do the same for me."

"If you had an orchard."

"Or if I needed help." The look in his eyes was faraway. Remembering...brooding. His forehead creased into a frown. "How will we pick apples with a baby around?"

"I'll think of something," Laurie said quickly.

She looked down at Cooper with one arm wrapped around the smooth bark of the tree and hoped against hope that they could pull it off, pick the apples, take care of Morgan, save the crop and the farm, too. And that she wouldn't lose her head or her heart in the bargain.

She didn't know him, this man standing beneath her with his arms across his chest, but somehow she knew that if anyone could help her, it was Cooper. She was staring down at him, he was staring up at her. Was this any way to get the apples picked?

Finally he put one hand on the ladder and asked in a low voice, "Are you coming down or shall I come up?"

Laurie felt her limbs turn to jelly. There was something so seductive about his voice, about the way he looked at her as if he might come up the ladder and pick her like a ripe apple. She gulped and unwrapped her arm from the tree. Then she dangled one foot in the general direction of the top rung of the ladder. But she couldn't find it. She reached for a branch, but it snapped off in her hand. And she felt herself falling, branches scratching her arms until she landed with an unceremonious whoosh in the arms of Cooper Buckingham and knocked him to the ground.

The world spun around in dizzying confusion, but when she opened her eyes she was lying on top of him, her breasts pressed against his rock-hard chest, her pelvic bones locked against his. Her hair had come loose from the rubber band and was fanned out across his cheek.

"I'm terribly sorry about this," she gasped, trying to raise herself off him. But she didn't have the strength. She fell back onto him, her face cradled against his collarbone.

"Are you hurt?" he asked in a hollow voice.

"I'm fine," she assured him. "I just can't move."

"Then don't," he advised, wrapping his arms around her, his hands splayed across her round, firm bottom.

But she did move. She had to. She couldn't stay that way, resting on top of him forever, his hands moving along the side of her thighs, causing tremors to race up and down her legs. She rolled off him. "Did I hurt you?" she asked with an anxious glance into his dark, penetrating eyes.

He shook his head, then reached out to tuck a strand of hair behind her ear. "When I told you to come down, I didn't mean without the ladder."

"I know." She was going to explain how it happened as soon as he took his hand away from her hair, as soon as he stopped looking at her as if she was a juicy McIntosh apple he'd like to bite into, when someone shouted at her from across the field. Only then was she able to get to her knees and let Cooper help her to her feet, her very unsteady feet.

"It's Gretel's new foreman," she explained, brushing the dirt off her pants. He's going to work part-time year-round and full-time during the harvest. He said he'd come by today." Her voice shook slightly.

The grizzled old man met them halfway across the orchard. "Glad I found you," he said, tipping his cap to Laurie. "I knocked on your back door but all's I heard was a baby crying."

Laurie's mouth flew open in alarm. "Oh, no, Morgan." She shot Cooper a desperate look. "Would you mind, just for a minute, while I talk to Mr. Ames?"

He didn't say yes and he didn't say no, he just shrugged and walked toward the house. Of course she could have gone herself and left Cooper with Mr. Ames, but he didn't know what to ask and she did. And then there was the fact that Cooper was better able to deal with Morgan than she was. She watched him go then turned her attention to the picking and packing of apples for market.

The cries reached Coop's ears as he neared the house. Unforgettably, unmistakably Morgan. He sprinted down the long hall to her bedroom, having no idea what he'd do when he got there. As it turned out, he didn't have to do anything. Just stand there. As soon as she saw him, Morgan stopped crying, waved her hands enthusiastically and fairly begged to be picked up.

But he didn't want to pick her up. Didn't know how to pick her up. Besides she might be wet or hungry. Or both. He stared down at her and she cooed and smiled up at him. It was the smile that did it. He had no choice. She knew how to get to him. He reached for her and picked her up with two hands, like a football, and held her out in front of him.

"Hello, Morgan," he said, looking into her pale blue eyes. "How are you?"

She chortled as if he'd just said something witty and he felt a wave of pride. For making her laugh. For making her stop crying. "Don't tell me you need a clean diaper." She grinned toothlessly and he gritted his teeth. "Okay, you win. A clean diaper it is," he said under his breath. Still holding her like a football, a fragile football made of glass, he moved down the hall to the bathroom and set her down on a wide counter covered with a waterproof pad. Under the counter was a package of disposable diapers. With one hand he unsnapped the soft pink fuzzy sleeper she wore and held her with the other so she wouldn't roll off.

Then he pulled off the old wet diaper and slid a new one under her bottom, closing it shut with the tape provided. When he held her up in front of him, the diaper slid off onto the floor.

"What did I do wrong?" he asked with a puzzled frown.

Morgan kicked her legs. He put her back down and tried again. This time he wrapped the adhesive tape tightly and quickly stuffed her arms and legs back into the sleeper. He snapped her up again so she wouldn't lose the diaper and hoped for the best.

Exhausted, he leaned back against the wall and looked down at the baby. "Now what?" he asked her. He was trapped. He had to find Laurie, but he couldn't leave the baby here. She might start crying again and he couldn't stand to hear her cry. He guessed she probably knew that.

Then he'd have to take her with him. He carried Morgan back into her room where he found her backpack in her closet, put her in it, then swung the pack on his back and headed out to the orchard. The next time, however, *he'd* talk to the apple man and *Laurie* would take care of Morgan. Picking apples had to be a lot easier than taking care of a baby.

Laurie was standing under a tree while Mr. Ames explained the proper picking procedure when the man suddenly looked up and said, "Here comes your husband."

Startled to see Morgan riding on Cooper's back, she said, "He's not my husband."

"Your baby then."

"No. My friend's."

"Your friend's husband, too?" he asked, looking puzzled.

"No. No one's husband." She took a deep breath. "My friend's baby and my friend's orchard. That's why I don't know anything about picking apples. Or anything about men," she muttered under her breath. Cooper was striding purposefully toward her, no doubt anxious to get rid of Morgan. But Morgan looked positively delighted to be bouncing along on Cooper's back. "I'm Gretel's...Mrs. Lundgren's friend. That's why I'm here," she said, making one last attempt to explain.

"Everything okay?" Laurie asked anxiously, lifting Morgan out of the backpack.

"Just wonderful," he said sarcastically. "I changed her diaper," he added.

"Thank you," she breathed. "Mr. Ames, here, was just explaining how to pick apples."

"Just telling your wife, here." He stopped and scratched his head. "I mean your friend's wife, or is it your wife's friend, that you got to gently cup each apple, then lift and twist it like so." He paused and twisted an apple off a low-hanging branch. "That way the apples'll stay fresh longer and the new buds will grow on the tree next year."

"Cup, lift and twist," Coop repeated. "I got it."

"Quick learner," Mr. Ames said, raising an eyebrow in Cooper's direction.

"Amazing," Coop said with a self-deprecating flash of humor. "I learned to change a diaper and pick an apple and the day isn't over yet." He stared off thoughtfully at the acres of trees that seemed to go on forever. "What about a machine?" he asked. "Wouldn't that work better?"

"Some growers use mechanical pickers," Mr. Ames said, "that shake the fruit from the tree. But those apples are used for applesauce and juice."

Coop shook his head with a smile. "I mean for changing diapers."

Mr. Ames stroked his chin for a moment. "Well, if you folks need any advice, about picking apples that is, let me know." With a nod he walked slowly across the field to his truck parked on the road outside the property, shaking his grizzled head as he went at the odd threesome who looked like a family but weren't. Who didn't look at all like apple pickers . . . but were.

Laurie rested Morgan on one hip and stared off after Mr. Ames, stifling the urge to call him back. To tell him she hadn't understood a word of what he said about scooping, lifting and twisting. Even if she had, how could they do anything, how could they even make a dent on this orchard with its acres of green, red and yellow apples, without the full complement of workers who were working elsewhere for the next two weeks.

Cooper seemed just as baffled as she was. Only instead of staring at the retreating figure of the apple expert, he was staring at her, as if she had a clue about what to do next.

"Well," she said, shifting Morgan to the other hip. "Shall we get started?"

Cooper looked at her as if she'd suggested they roll over the Falls in a barrel. He let his gaze sweep across the endless fruit trees then come back to Laurie. "Sure," he said. "What are you going to do with...her?" He jerked his thumb in Morgan's direction.

Laurie had the feeling he'd almost said "it" instead of "her." But she wasn't here to quibble, to wonder at Cooper's lack of interest in babies. She was there to pick apples. She frowned. "I don't know," she confessed. "I was thinking of bringing out her playpen."

"And she'd play while we worked?"

She nodded, trying to ignore his skeptical tone. True, Morgan had not shown a desire to amuse herself, but they had to try. With every passing minute an apple somewhere was rotting on the tree and Gretel and Steve were losing money. They went into the house. They found the playpen and carried it and Morgan out to the orchard. The air was crisp and cool and the autumn sun slanted through the leaves of the trees. Laurie put Morgan in the playpen and surrounded her with her favorite toys, including her troll. Then Laurie tiptoed to the nearest tree and reached for a low-hanging apple, hoping Morgan wouldn't notice they'd gone back to work.

After an anxious glance over her shoulder at the baby, Laurie tried to concentrate on cupping, lifting and twisting apples and placing them carefully into a bin. Cooper was high on top of the ladder, placing apples into a canvas bag hanging from his shoulder. Laurie peered up at him through the branches, noticing the intent expression on his face and the way the sun backlit his head and broad shoulders, thinking of how strange it was to be working alongside a man she'd never seen before last week, a man she couldn't seem to tear her eyes away from now.

He paused to inspect an apple and caught her eye. "What is it?" he asked.

"Nothing." Laurie reached for an apple, embarrassed to be caught staring. "I was just thinking this isn't such a bad life." She extended her arms. "Fresh air, all the apples you can eat."

"All the apples you can *pick,*" he said dryly. "I'll ask you again what you think of this life after a week or so."

Laurie braced her arm against the tree. "A week or so! You're not going to be here that long. By that time Gretel and Steve will be home and there'll be professional pickers here."

"I hope so," he said. "For our friends' sake. Because you're the slowest picker I've ever seen." He looked pointedly at the near-empty bin on the ground next to Laurie and she flushed guiltily.

"I know, I know," she admitted, grabbing an apple off the tree, and then another. After she'd carefully made one layer of shiny green apples in the bottom of the bin, she paused. "How many other pickers have you seen, anyway?"

He answered without breaking his rhythm. Cup, lift, twist. "I don't have to see any to know you're the slowest." In his haste Cooper dropped an apple and it fell to the ground. Laurie gave him a pointed look and he responded with a disarming grin. Maybe he was having a good time, she thought. Maybe he was tired of slugging it out with the Falls. Was that really why he was here, to take a break? To relax in the peace and quiet of an orchard?

But Morgan wasn't about to let anyone relax. She'd had enough of her troll, her alphabet blocks and Raggedy Ann doll and she wanted some attention. She started slowly by throwing her troll over the side of the playpen and then making helpless little sounds to let them know she wanted it back. Laurie picked faster, knowing her time was almost up. When Morgan's pitiful cries had turned to full-fledged wails and Cooper was glaring at her from behind the branches, Laurie sighed and went to pick up her charge.

No sooner was Morgan in Laurie's arms when she stretched her arms up toward Cooper. "Maybe she needs something to eat," Laurie said hopefully, knowing it would take something special to keep her mind off Cooper. He nodded and went on picking. After all, Laurie thought as she walked back to the house with Morgan in her arms, he'd volunteered to pick, not entertain Morgan. If only Morgan understood that.

Once Laurie had the baby in her high chair and had tempted her with applesauce, yogurt and apple juice, Morgan showed her what she thought of her attempts to pacify her by sweeping all of the items off the tray and onto the floor.

"Morgan," Laurie said, sighing deeply, "is this any way to win friends? Remember there are some people who don't find this kind of behavior attractive. You're lucky those people aren't around now, but if you cry any louder they'll hear you. Do you know what I'm saying?'' Laurie asked, pressing her face against Morgan's little button nose.

Morgan gulped back a sob and grabbed a handful of Laurie's hair. ''Ouch,'' Laurie cried. ''Let go, Morgan, or I'll tell your mother on you.''

Just then Laurie felt a draft from the kitchen door behind her. Wrenching her hair from Morgan's grasp she swiveled around and saw Cooper framed in the doorway. ''Do you think it's a good idea to threaten her?'' he asked, closing the door behind him. ''What would Dr. Spock say?''

''I don't know what he'd say,'' she said, bending over to clean up the mess on the floor. ''And right now I don't really care. All I know is that this child is trying my patience. To the max. She won't eat. She won't do anything.''

As soon as she'd uttered the words Laurie realized Cooper had taken her place at the table and was spooning heaping mouthfuls of yogurt into Morgan's mouth. Morgan was actually smacking her lips in delight. Of course. Laurie should have known. Whatever Cooper did, Morgan loved. Laurie sighed and continued her cleanup job, watching out of the corner of her eye while Cooper continued to shovel more food into Morgan's mouth.

Laurie finally got to her feet and decided it was time for a coffee break. She couldn't stand there watching them, fantasizing that this was her family, that this big man and tiny girl encompassed her life here on the farm. She had to get on with the job, then get away and find her own husband, one who wanted children and then have some.

Maybe she couldn't have an orchard or a bed and breakfast like her sister's Miramar Inn in California, but she could have something. But only if she didn't stop choosing the wrong men. And Cooper Buckingham, despite what Morgan thought of him, was about as wrong as they got. He took temporary jobs, had no intention of settling down, getting married and most definitely did not want children.

But for the moment Laurie needed him. Needed him to pick apples and to amuse Morgan. Needed him to keep her company, to keep her from going crazy with worry over the orchard, the apple crop and Morgan. She didn't know why he was still there, hanging in there, when the work was backbreaking and Morgan was irritable. She suspected he was here to help out Steve, but she couldn't help hoping there was another reason.

As she measured the coffee into the filter, Laurie carefully phrased a question for Cooper, even though she knew he didn't like talking about himself. "Do you, uh...have any brothers or sisters?" she asked. Maybe that was why he was so good with kids. If he had been a baby-sitter for half a dozen little siblings, that would explain it.

"I'm an only child," he said brusquely.

"Then I don't see... I mean how you can be so..."

"I don't either. Let's not worry about it, okay? Just believe me when I say I don't know anything about kids. I'm not interested in them, don't want any and don't know any. Except Morgan here.''

At the mention of her name Morgan hit the end of her spoon handle on her tray and sent it flying, spattering Cooper's shirt with strawberry yogurt. Laurie squeezed her eyes shut hoping it would all be cleaned up when she opened them, but it wasn't. Cooper was still sitting at the table staring at Morgan in disbelief, with a strange look on his face while he tried to decide how to react. If Laurie hadn't known him better she would have sworn he was going to laugh. But he didn't. Without saying a word, he got up from the table, went out the back door to his car and came back with a duffel bag in his hand.

Panic rose in her throat. "Are you leaving?" she asked shakily.

"I'm changing," he announced.

Laurie exhaled a ragged breath. "I'm really sorry about this," she said. "And so is Morgan."

"She doesn't look sorry," Cooper noted dryly.

Laurie willed Morgan to look sorry, to miraculously say her first word, to make that word be sorry. But she didn't. She crumbled crackers in her tiny fist and threw the crumbs on the floor.

Cooper walked out of the kitchen and down the hall in the direction of the guest room to change. The yogurt was beginning to dry into stains on his shirt. The apples were out there waiting to be picked and two adults were devoting their time and energy to one little bombshell with no manners at all. The whole situation was crazy. He should never have come. Besides the frustrating situation, the sight of Morgan in the high chair was painful. It brought back too many memories of an empty high chair, an empty house and his empty life.

If he were smart he'd get out of Laurie Clayton's life immediately. But if he were smart he'd never have gotten into it in the first place. Because now he was in the middle of a crisis, an apple crisis that couldn't possibly be solved by two inexperienced adults who couldn't even take care of one baby.

He tossed his bag onto the bed as if he lived there— as if he belonged there—and found a clean shirt. That was the trouble, he thought, looking around the room decorated with Native American weavings on the wall and pictures of the Great Lakes: he was too much at home here. He didn't want a home. Or a wife or a baby. Ever again. But this was no time for painful memories. No time to envy a friend for his life. Not when there was work to be done, a baby to be entertained and a beautiful woman in the kitchen waiting for him, depending on him.

She was waiting with a cup of coffee, laced with cream. He looked up questioningly.

"Is that right, cream and no sugar?" she asked.

He nodded. "But how did you know?"

"That first night. After you made dinner, I made coffee."

He nodded with a provocative smile. "The day you picked me up."

She lifted Morgan out of her high chair and rested her chin on Morgan's soft curls. "I didn't pick you up, you picked *me* up. Who came and sat down at our table?" she asked.

"Who dropped her troll?" he said.

"It certainly wasn't me. And it certainly wasn't her. And it certainly wasn't on purpose. I guess you think I go around using Morgan to pick up men all the time." Her hazel eyes sparkled indignantly.

He shrugged. "It worked."

She sat down with Morgan in her lap while he stood at the kitchen cabinet looking down at her. "It didn't work. If I'd been trying to pick up somebody, it wouldn't have been you."

"You really know how to hurt a guy," he said, noticing the way her cheeks flamed with color when she was agitated.

"I'm sorry," she said contritely while Morgan wriggled in her arms. "I didn't mean that. But...you know what I mean."

"I know what you mean," he said. "You're looking for a man you can count on. One who wants to get married and have kids, right?"

"Is it that obvious?"

"It's what most women want," he said.

"And what most men don't."

"I don't know about that," he said, folding his arms across his chest as Morgan reached out in his direction. He didn't want to hold her, didn't want to feel her baby-soft cheek against his, to imagine what it would be like...

"I know about it," Laurie answered, "or I should after what I've been through. What I don't understand is why. Marriage is such a good deal for men. Maybe you can explain it to me?"

"No, I can't," he said firmly, terminating the conversation before they got in any deeper, any more personal. "We've got apples to pick, bins to fill and miles to go before we sleep."

Chapter Five

By the end of the day they'd only filled five bins from one and a half trees, and placed the bins by the side of the road for the local trucker to pick up. It was cheering and disheartening at the same time to see that the farm workers' bins were stacked to an impressive height alongside of their puny pile. But Laurie and Cooper had taken time out to eat an apple, soothe Morgan when she fussed, picked up every toy she'd thrown out of the playpen and watched while she fell asleep under her blanket. Then and only then did they enjoy an hour of uninterrupted work and quiet.

They didn't mar the silence by talking. They just picked, silently and steadily. Laurie didn't want to continue the discussion about what women and men wanted, and she was sure Cooper didn't, either.

It was pointless. They both knew each other's views and they couldn't be farther apart. If only Laurie didn't always want what she couldn't have. It was a severe character flaw, one she thought she could overcome until she met Cooper. Now if only she could keep her mind on apples and forget how his body fit so perfectly with hers, when she'd fallen on top of him earlier. If only she could stop staring at him, wondering if he'd ever kiss her again. Wondering if it was really as wonderful as she remembered.

When dusk fell, Cooper gathered their equipment and Laurie gathered Morgan and went back to the house. She put the little girl in her windup swing and stood staring hypnotically as the baby swung back and forth. Laurie's back ached, she was tired and hungry. She heard Cooper open the refrigerator and like Pavlov's dog, her mouth watered.

"Did you find anything?" she asked hopefully, coming up behind him and peering over his shoulder.

"What about chicken curry with apple chutney?" he asked, turning to face her.

Her eyes widened. "I thought all you could make was hamburgers."

"I found the chutney in the fridge and a container labeled Chicken Curry in the freezer. Think it's okay if we eat it?"

"Of course. Gretel would want us to. I might even figure out how to make rice to go with it."

"You really don't know how to cook?" he asked.

She shook her head slowly. "I know what you're thinking. No wonder I'm single." She sighed. "Maybe you're right. I ought to take some lessons."

With the refrigerator still open, he looked at her for a long moment until she had to reach for the counter to steady herself. The intensity of his gaze left her weak-kneed.

"Don't do that," he said at last. "Stay the way you are. Most guys don't care as much about cooking as..."

She waited patiently but he never finished his sentence. Instead he looked at her with a mixture of regret and blatant desire that made her pulse race. She forgot about the curry and the chutney, she forgot everything but Cooper until the cold air finally brought her out of her trance and he closed the refrigerator.

"Can I help?" she asked as he turned his back on her and went to the stove.

"You can see if there are any condiments."

"Condiments...sure." She walked into Gretel's pantry and scanned the shelves, trying to get her runaway emotions under control. Unless she did, this wasn't going to work, this apple picking, this togetherness. She was weak, she was vulnerable and she was infatuated with this man.

Cooper stayed at the sink until she'd left the room. Could she help? she asked. She could help by not standing so close to him, so close he could see the green flecks in her hazel eyes and notice the shape of her lips inviting him to kiss her again. She had no idea how desirable she was, no idea how hard it was to keep from lifting her up onto the counter, cupping the back of her head with his palm and inhaling the smell of ripe apples that clung to her skin and devouring her with his mouth. She had that effect on him and God help him he was having trouble resisting her scent, her taste and her touch.

But he had to. Since the accident two years ago he'd been on the run. Running from his memories. His sorrow. He'd had a dozen or more assignments. They'd been interesting. There'd been an occasional woman who'd also been interesting, but not interesting enough to pick apples for, to drive around Buffalo in the rain for and to feed a baby yogurt for. If he wasn't careful this interest could lead to a relationship he didn't want. Not with any woman. And definitely not with a woman like Laurie. The kind who'd been hurt once and was only interested in playing for keeps. Just the sight of her with Morgan in her arms should have been enough to send him running for the door.

But he wasn't running. Instead he was thawing curry, sipping sherry he'd gotten from the liquor cabinet and listening to some mellow jazz on the local radio while Morgan dozed in her swing. It all felt so natural he could almost imagine himself belonging there. But it was only Morgan who belonged there. The rest of them were just visitors. He moved to the pantry door where Laurie was standing, staring at the shelves, the overhead light shining on her golden hair.

"What have you got there?" he asked, taking her hand and uncurling her fingers from a box of raisins. Her hand was warm and felt slightly rough from the day's work. You look tired," he said, taking the raisins and running his thumb around her palm. "Why don't you relax in a hot bath?"

She nodded and her eyelashes were shadowed against her cheeks. "What about you?" she murmured.

"Somebody has to stay and watch the curry."

"I just meant..."

He knew what she meant, but the sudden vision of joining her in a giant tub of hot water sent his heart pounding with anticipation.

"I'll put Morgan to bed," she said. She tried to walk around him but he blocked her way in the small pantry. She put her hand on his shoulder and he backed her against the wall and pinned her there with his hands on her arms.

"Laurie," he said in a low voice. "I just want you to know I... Oh, God what am I trying to say?"

The expectant look in her eyes, her lightly parted lips, her silky hair clinging to her cheek stole his breath away and with it the words he wanted to say. "I understand," she murmured.

"No, you don't," he countered and then he kissed her. He couldn't help it. The pantry was so warm and so still, with jars of applesauce and applejuice gleaming from the shelves and she was so achingly sweet, so tempting. She didn't resist. She wrapped her arms around his neck as if she was waiting for this moment. She kissed him with a hunger that matched his own. Not once, not twice, but over and over as if that made it all right, when they both knew it wasn't. Finally she broke away and held him at arm's length, gazing deeply into his eyes, searching for answers.

"You're right," she murmured in a shaky voice. "I don't understand." Then she bolted for the door, gently scooped up Morgan out of her swing, put her to bed and then finally, at last headed for Gretel's room and the master bath.

Cooper stood for a long moment breathing hard. How could she possibly understand what was going on when he didn't, either? All he knew was that he wanted her the way he never thought he'd want a woman again. But that didn't mean he had to do anything about it.

Oh, yeah? he heard an inner voice say. It sure looked as though he was doing "something" about it. He shook his head and closed the pantry door behind him. It couldn't go any further. Cooper was there to pick apples and that was all. Okay, maybe cook a few meals because if he didn't, they'd starve, but definitely no more kissing in the pantry.

Speaking of starving, he read the instructions from the back of a package of rice and measured out the ingredients. He had no confidence that Laurie could make rice. He didn't really care if she could boil water. Raiding the pantry once more he came up with a jar of artichoke hearts, a can of garbanzo beans and some brine-cured olives and he threw them all together for a salad.

The memories of other dinners, another home, came flooding back unexpectedly and he clamped his lips together and fought back tears he hadn't shed for years. Why had the memories resurfaced now? Was it Morgan, Laurie or this house? He wished Laurie would come back and take his mind off the past. He wondered if she'd fallen asleep in the tub. He wondered with a quickening heartbeat if he ought to make a quick check.

But as it turned out, he didn't have to. She came back into the kitchen, fresh from a bath, wearing clean jeans and a T-shirt just as the phone began to ring.

Laurie grabbed the phone on the kitchen wall. "Gretel, how are you?"

"Wonderful," her friend answered. "How's Morgan?"

"Just fine," Laurie said, watching Cooper stir a pot on the stove. The walls of her stomach rubbed together. Lunch seemed like an awfully long time ago. As Gretel recounted her day's activities, Laurie watched the back of Cooper's neck, studied the way his hair brushed the collar of his shirt, and when he suddenly turned and smiled at her she lost her train of thought completely.

"Sorry," she said, suddenly realizing she hadn't heard a word Gretel had said. "How did you say you liked the hotel?"

"I didn't say," Gretel said. "I was telling you about the outdoor salmon barbecue on the island."

"Of course," Laurie said. "So you're having a good time?"

"Marvelous. Steve's out renting a tandem bicycle for us right now. But what about you? I feel so guilty, having fun while you're back there all alone."

"Well, actually I'm not alone." She glanced at Cooper who paused to give her a sideways glance that made her heart race. How could she explain about Cooper when he was right there in the room listening to every word she said? How could she explain about Cooper under any circumstances? "You won't believe this but Steve's old friend Cooper Buckingham is here."

"Cooper Buckingham, the one who works at the Falls?" Gretel asked.

"Yes, that one."

"What's he doing there?" Gretel demanded.

"Doing?" Laurie asked absently, trying to stop staring, to stop imagining how it would be if *they* lived there, if this were *their* kitchen, *their* baby in the nursery. "Oh, cooking—cooking dinner." She didn't dare say picking apples or Gretel would worry.

"But, but Cooper's a recluse, hasn't been heard from since... He's one of Steve's best friends, you know. He's the one I wanted you to meet."

"Yes, I know. Well, you just go off and have a great bike ride. And don't worry about a thing."

"I won't. But Laurie—well, I'll call you later, when we can talk."

"Yes, do that." Laurie hung up with a sigh of relief and turned to Cooper.

"What did she say?" he asked.

"They're having a great time." She lifted the lid on the pot of curry and inhaled deeply. "Going bike riding."

"I mean about me being here."

"She was surprised."

"I'll bet. I haven't seen much of Steve or Gretel over the years, and suddenly I'm in his house cooking dinner." He looked around the kitchen as if he, too, was more than a little surprised at where he was and what he was doing. "She must have wondered why."

Laurie placed her hands on her hips, watching the steam swirl up out of the pot. "Even I wonder why," she confessed.

He shrugged. "Because I want to help. I owe it to Steve."

Laurie nodded. Nothing about her, about wanting to help *her,* spend time with her. Of course not. She must not even imagine it or she was heading for disappointment bordering on depression. "But the job is overwhelming, even with the workers we've got. Doesn't that discourage you?"

"Sure, sometimes. It would be a lot easier without Morgan, you know."

"What do you suggest we do with her, put her in day care?" she asked.

"Of course not. I was just stating the obvious. I'm sorry."

Touched by his apology, Laurie put her hand on his arm. "I understand. I must confess I had no idea what having a baby on your hands entailed. It's not quite the way I pictured it, the crying, the teething."

"But it hasn't discouraged you," he asked. "You still want one of your own?"

Laurie shrugged as if it didn't matter one way or the other. But it did. She wanted a baby. A baby of her own. To love, to nurture, to hold next to her heart through teething and crying and colic. Yes, she wanted a baby. But what she wanted and what she had were two different things. She didn't want to go into that with Cooper. He was only being polite. It didn't really matter to him if she had a baby or not. She went to the silverware drawer and picked out forks and knives, running her fingers across the raised rose pattern.

"You're lucky," she said. "You know exactly what you want and you've got it."

Cooper didn't answer. If she'd said that a week ago he would have agreed. Now he wasn't so sure. It was Laurie's fault. She'd made him want *her* and staying with her in the charming old house had stirred feelings that he'd buried years ago. He didn't like being reminded of what he'd lost and he didn't like being tempted by a woman who was looking for something he couldn't give.

Instead of saying something, he heated the curry, tossed the salad and when he turned around he found Laurie had set the kitchen table and was pouring water into tall glasses with a thoughtful expression. He wanted to tell Laurie it was nothing personal, these feelings he had. He didn't have anything against Morgan or her. In fact Morgan had many delightful moments. So delightful he almost envied her parents. He wanted to tell Laurie he'd once wanted children as badly as she did. But he'd closed the door on that part of his life. Didn't think about it, didn't talk about it. He couldn't if he wanted to survive.

He didn't talk during dinner and neither did Laurie. It was as if a cloud had descended and hovered over the plain pinewood table. It wasn't the food. The curry was excellent—not too spicy, not too bland. It was the atmosphere, so homey... and yet... it wasn't their home. It was also the look in Laurie's eyes that made him sad for her and for himself. They had to stop acting like a family. He had to stop kissing Lau-

rie in the pantry and stop rolling around with her under the apple trees. Yes, he had to stop before it was
too late. Before he did something they'd both regret.

He pushed his chair away from the table. "I'm going to fix the strap on the bag. It's almost ripped
through," he said abruptly before he walked out of the
kitchen.

Laurie stared after him. There was something wrong
with him tonight. And he was not the type to confide
in her and tell her what was bothering him. Laurie
washed the dishes and went to check on Morgan. She
was sleeping soundly.

"Picking apples is hard work, right, Morgan?" she
murmured to the baby before she left the nursery.
Taking care of a baby *and* picking apples was even
harder. Throw in trying to fathom Cooper Buckingham and you had your work cut out for you.

Laurie peered out into the dark night looking for a
light in the garage or the barn. But there was none.
Maybe he'd left. Maybe he was gone for good. She
couldn't blame him if he was. Whatever obligation he
felt toward Steve, he'd fulfilled it. He no longer had
any real reason to hang around. Yes, he could pick
more apples, and every little bit helped. But he didn't
like children and Morgan was a handful even for those
who did and wanted one of their own. Then there was
the strange attraction between them that neither
wanted. Yes, if she were Cooper she'd be out of there
like a shot, too. But without a word or even a note?

Laurie grabbed a flashlight from the drawer and
ventured out the front door heading off between rows
of heavily-laden apple trees, trying to stay calm, try-

ing not to panic. If he was gone she'd deal with it. She'd pick what she could and take care of Morgan as best she could. She tried not to think of the solitary meals, of the lack of stimulating conversation, the absence of his physical presence that had such a disturbing effect on her, of his sideways glance, the touch of his hands and the warmth of his kisses.

He'd leave sooner or later anyway and it might as well be sooner and give her time to get used to it. Suddenly there was a smell in the air that brought back memories of her childhood. It was cigar smoke.

"Who's there?" she asked, waving her light in a wide arc.

"Just me," Cooper said, looming out of the darkness.

She breathed a sigh of relief as her light picked up the outline of Cooper's tall form, the spiral of smoke and the rich aroma of his cigar.

"Do you mind?" he said with a look at the cigar.

She shook her head. "It reminds me of my dad," she said, switching off her flashlight. "He used to smoke on holidays and special occasions."

"Not any more?"

"He died a few years ago. My sister and I are the only ones left. I suppose that's why we're so close. We lived together at the bed-and-breakfast she owns before she got married. She says I'll always have a home there and it's a wonderful place, on the California coast, very romantic with the surf crashing against the rocks beneath the house. The Miramar Inn is booked for weeks in advance. And now to top it off, she's expecting a baby." She smiled ruefully. "Babies all around me. You'll think I'm obsessed with them. One of these days I'll pull myself together and go back to work."

"For the airline?"

"No, I don't think so."

"Picking apples?" He smiled at her.

"It would probably get boring after a while," she said with a smile of her own.

"Sometimes it's good to do mindless physical work," he said. "It gives you time to think. Other times you don't want to think at all."

"Is this one of those times?" she asked, trying to make out his expression in the dark.

He paused for a long moment. She really couldn't see his face. She could only see the glowing light from the end of his cigar, but she could imagine the lines furrowed in his forehead as he pondered the question.

"This is one of those times," he admitted, "when I'd rather not think. Tell me about your job with the airline." He sat down under a tree and beckoned her to do the same.

She sank down next to him on a ground cover of leaves and leaned back against the trunk of the tree. Maybe it was the dark night, the brush of his arm against hers or the rustle of the leaves above them, but once she started talking she couldn't seem to stop. She even talked about Roger and the more she talked the less it hurt. She told him about cities she'd stayed in and strange encounters with strange passengers.

Cooper listened, chuckled and smoked his cigar in appreciative silence. When she finally ran out of

breath and stories, and her spine was stiff and her
bottom sore, she tried to read her watch in the dark.
"It's late," she said at last. "I must have talked your
ear off."

"Not quite," he said, standing and reaching for her
hand to pull her up beside him. He dusted the leaves
off her curved fanny and the touch of his hand made
her want to wrap her arms around him. She was so
tired and he was so rock solid. She reminded herself he
was just being helpful, friendly. That was all. His hand
rested on the curve of her hip as they walked back to
the house without speaking.

She said good-night to him in the living room then
left to check on Morgan. She didn't want to leave him.
She wanted to prolong the intimacy that had made her
pour out her stories, her memories. But she couldn't
trust herself, not at this hour of the night. She was too
vulnerable, too emotionally spent to trust herself another minute with him. If he kissed her she wouldn't
resist. She'd kiss him back. If he held her she would
cling to him and never let him go. That's how weak she
was. She wasn't proud of herself for forgetting her
long-term goals in favor of instant gratification, but
she chalked it off to the hour, the fatigue and the underlying tension between them that was always there.

The next day Laurie dragged her stiff, aching body
out of bed. She and Cooper had a simple breakfast of
toast and coffee and they continued where they'd left
off the previous day in the orchard. Morgan didn't last
long in her playpen. Her pitiful cries earned her a place
on Cooper's back. He said he could pick faster if he

didn't have to hear her crying. Laurie watched with admiration as he moved up and down the ladder, emptying his canvas sack.

Gretel called around noon when they were sitting under a tree having lunch. Laurie made sandwiches and brought them to the orchard, along with the portable phone.

"Can you talk?" was the first thing Gretel asked.

Laurie took a deep breath. "Here's the situation," she began. "We're having a picnic in the orchard."

"We ... who's we?" Gretel demanded.

"Your friend Cooper, Morgan and me."

"How romantic," Gretel said, gushing.

"Yes and no," Laurie said, looking at Cooper who was lounging on his side on the plaid blanket, his head propped in his hand, a blade of grass between his teeth. He was staring off into space as if she wasn't there while Morgan dozed peacefully in the dappled sunlight. "I mean I don't want you to get the wrong idea."

"Heavens no. Steve wants to talk to Cooper, but he's in the shower now. So he'll have to do it later. Suffice it to say that he was surprised to hear you two had connected. Knowing Cooper... Well, what do you think of him? Isn't he divine?"

"Of course," Laurie said carefully. "But I thought..."

"You thought I didn't know him. I don't really, though he came to our wedding. Steve wanted him to be Morgan's godfather, but under the circumstances..."

Circumstances? What circumstances? Darn it, why did Gretel always have to call when Cooper was around? "Maybe you can tell me about it later," she suggested.

"Maybe he'll tell you himself."

"I don't think so," Laurie said with a glance at Cooper's impassive face. The chances of Cooper telling her anything about anything seemed remote at that point.

"So...is he actually staying there, at the house with you?" Gretel asked. "I mean can't you tell me something, anything? I—*we're*—dying of curiosity."

Laurie smiled at the frustration in her friend's voice. "Not really. It's a long story. Have a wonderful time," she said and hung up.

Cooper's gaze met hers and she realized he'd been listening to every word. "What did she say?" he asked.

"Steve wanted to talk to you, but he was in the shower."

"Good."

"Good that he wants to talk to you or good he was in the shower?"

Cooper tossed aside the blade of grass.

"Both. If he talks to me he'll want to dredge up old times."

"Is that so bad?" she asked, folding the tablecloth at the edges.

"I prefer to live in the present."

"Of course. And it's better you don't talk to him. You might let it slip about the apples."

A smile quirked one corner of his mouth. "You think I can't keep a secret?"

She stared at his mouth, remembering the touch of his lips on hers, wondering . . . wishing he would kiss her again, but knowing that something stood in their way, something in the past, some *circumstances*. Sometimes she just wanted to blurt it out, to ask him what happened; other times she was afraid to find out. "I think you're good at keeping secrets," she said soberly. "All I know about you is that you're an only child. I don't even know if you have a family or where they are."

"I have two parents," he admitted. "They live in South Carolina."

Where they're waiting hopelessly for a grandchild, Laurie thought. She knew how pleased her parents would be if they were alive to know about her sister's pregnancy.

Cooper gave Laurie a long look that told her he knew exactly what she was doing—fishing for information. Prying into his private life. She was transparent. She knew it, but she didn't care. Before long Steve and Gretel would be home and she could ask them. But Cooper would leave and she'd never see him again.

She'd miss him. She'd miss this life, this sharing of food, work and conversation. But he probably wouldn't give her a thought when he left. He'd probably be glad to get away from the backbreaking work, the fussy baby and from herself with her questions about a past he'd rather forget.

"They must be proud of you," she said. It was her last attempt to continue the conversation.

"Why?" he asked, raising one eyebrow.

"Well, because you're so successful, so good at what you do."

"But that's all."

"That's all you want, isn't it?"

"Yes," he said emphatically and climbed back up the ladder to resume picking while Laurie carried the picnic basket back to the house. What was he thinking? she wondered. What were the "circumstances" in his life that Gretel had hinted about? She was pretty sure he wouldn't tell her, nor would he want her to know, but that didn't stop her from trying to figure out what made Cooper Buckingham tick.

Chapter Six

"Doesn't your back hurt?" Laurie asked Cooper the next morning as she got up from the breakfast table and rubbed one hip.

Cooper let his gaze linger on the sweet curve of her hip for just a moment. Then he shook his head. But his back felt as if he'd been sleeping on a bed of nails. It was the bending and stooping, the stretching with a twenty-pound baby on his back as well as a canvas sack full of apples over his shoulder. If he admitted it, Laurie would put Morgan back in her playpen where she'd cry or she'd try to carry her around herself.

"I'm fine," he assured her. "But I want to check in with my office. I never told them where I was going. I might have some messages."

"What if they want you back?" Laurie asked, worry lines forming between her eyebrows.

Cooper dialed his office number on the kitchen phone. What if they did want him back? He couldn't go. Couldn't leave the two of them in the lurch. Even though they were barely making a dent on the orchard. The support he gave was more psychological than anything, considering the number of apples he actually picked. But he couldn't tell his back that.

When his boss answered, he told Cooper there was a crack in the pen-stock. "Not that it's your problem anymore. Where are you anyway?"

"Taking a few days off in the country," Cooper explained. "How big is it?"

"Not that big, but I want to stop it now, before it gets any bigger. I know you're finished here and you did a fine job, too," the older man said gruffly. "But is there any way you could get back here and help us out? I don't want to have to shut it off."

Cooper frowned. Shutting off the power would mean a loss of revenue, a big blow to the power company. "I might be able to design something with steel straps. I don't know, I can't promise anything."

"You mean you'll come? You'll give it a shot?"

Cooper glanced at Laurie who was standing at the sink listening, the breakfast dishes forgotten. "All right. But only as long as it takes to fix the crack, then I have to get back here."

"Thanks, Cooper, I knew you wouldn't let us down."

When he hung up, Laurie turned off the water and removed her rubber gloves without turning around. "You're leaving," she said with a catch in her voice.

"Not for long. I'll be back tonight if all goes well."

She nodded, but her shoulders slumped.

He crossed the room in two strides and put his hands firmly on her shoulders. "Don't even think about picking apples without me."

"I have to," she said, matching his determined tone.

"You can't. Not with Morgan on your hands."

"There must be a way," she said. There was grim determination in her voice.

"There is no way. Take the day off," he insisted. "Come with me." He turned her around to face him. "I'll drop you and Morgan at the viewing area if you promise to keep your keys in your purse."

She bit back a smile. "You must have thought I was a complete idiot," she said, closing her eyes for a moment to blot out the scene she knew she'd never forget.

"Not complete," he assured her.

"Oh, good. That's reassuring." One corner of her mouth tilted up in amusement despite herself.

He grinned at her and traced the outline of her cheek with his thumb. He hadn't known a thing about her that day at the Falls. Didn't know how patient she was with Morgan, how determined she was to save the orchard, how loyal she was to her friend. How beautiful, how classic her looks, how sexy... But he had known that then. Or suspected. The electricity between them had been there even then, had drawn him to her that first day, and continued to draw him closer even now.

She was still hesitating. "I feel so guilty," she said. "Gretel's counting on me."

"For what?"

"For taking care of Morgan, of course. But the orchard sort of fell in my lap."

"There you are. Morgan first. Morgan will enjoy a trip to the Falls." He didn't mention that on Morgan's last trip she'd cried nonstop. He only knew he didn't want to leave them alone, even for a day. Morgan, still in her high chair, smeared her oatmeal all over her face. As if to cast her vote in favor of another trip to the Falls, she clapped her sticky hands together. Laurie and Cooper exchanged an amused look.

Laurie gave a sigh of resignation. "All right, you win," she said.

Cooper wasn't sure if she was talking to him or to Morgan. "We all win," he said quickly before she changed her mind. "The Power Authority wins if I can solve the hydraulic problem and you...we...give our backs a rest and tomorrow we go back to the orchard. *And* you and Morgan get to see the sights you missed the first time around. I've got passes for the guided tour to the platform at the bottom of the Falls."

She hesitated only a moment before she nodded and went to pack Morgan's diaper bag.

Feeling euphoric, Cooper went to the guest room to get his jacket. Why he should feel this rush of adrenaline he wasn't sure. It was just another day at work for him, wasn't it? It couldn't be that he was getting attached to Laurie, could it? So attached he wouldn't be able to leave her at all? He shuddered at the thought.

Maybe he should have thought of that before he urged her to go with him today. Because he was suddenly aware that the more time he spent with her the more time he wanted to spend with her.

In the car it got worse. He had second thoughts and then third thoughts. The worrisome part was that it felt so natural to be driving around with a baby in the car seat behind him and a warm and lovely blond woman at his side. They talked easily about the weather and what the rain might do to the apples while his mind was in turmoil. They talked about the ordinary everyday things people talk about when they know each other very well. But he didn't know her very well. And yet he did know her. He knew what she wanted. Knew what she deserved. And it wasn't him.

He dropped her and Morgan in the parking lot. The same parking lot where he'd kissed her goodbye for good. He had an overwhelming desire to kiss her again. And not goodbye. But that was ridiculous. He'd be back in a few hours. And he wasn't that far gone that he had to kiss her every few hours. Not yet.

"Here are the tickets. Or if you don't want to take the tour, take a boat ride on the *Maid of the Mist*." He lifted Morgan out of her car seat and into the backpack on Laurie's back. "Behave," he instructed the baby. "No crying, understand?"

Morgan playfully grabbed his finger and bit it. He withdrew it and turned to Laurie. "If you get tired, go over to the hotel. I'll try to join you for lunch, okay?"

"Thanks. Don't worry about us. We'll be fine." She turned and made her way to the viewing area. Morgan craned her neck around in his direction and he grinned at her despite the teethmarks indented on his finger. He had to admit she was a cute kid, and bubbled over with personality. Not always the kind of personality that made her easy to handle, but a personality nonetheless. He stood staring after them until they disappeared in the crowd.

A gray-haired man with a grandfather twinkle in his eye caught Cooper's attention. "Nice baby," he observed.

"Thanks," Cooper said. "I mean . . ."

"You're a lucky man," he added with a trace of envy in his voice.

Cooper nodded politely. Lucky? If only the man knew he'd had the worst luck a man could live through.

At one o'clock Cooper looked up to find his neck was stiff and his brain was numb. He needed a break. His colleagues had temporarily slowed the leak to a dribble while he worked, so the sense of urgency he'd felt at first had diminished somewhat. He wondered where Laurie and Morgan were. Was Morgan screaming her head off in the dining room? Had she thrown something else into the tempestuous river? He turned off his computer, told everyone he would be back in an hour and drove to the hotel. He scanned the dining room, but they weren't there. He frowned. They should be hungry by now. Or had they already come and gone? He asked the maître d' if he'd noticed a woman with a baby, but he shook his head.

Cooper strode briskly across the road to the visitors' center, hit the snack bar and the gift shop, but Laurie and Morgan were nowhere to be seen. A tremor of anxiety hit him. He took the glass elevator to the observation platform, his heart pounding in his chest, and there, two hundred feet above the base of the gorge, he had a view of both falls— But no blond woman with a red-haired baby on her back, unless they were in the midst of the dozens of figures in yellow raincoats... There was no way to tell.

Why had he let them take off on their own? The churning, tumbling water usually soothed him, but today it seemed ominous, dangerous. He knew thousands of tourists visited the Falls every year and nothing happened to them, but they weren't his...friends. Cooper punched the Down button with his fist but after waiting an interminable thirty seconds, he ran down the five flights of stairs to the base and from there to the hurricane deck.

As his feet pounded the deck, the winds hit him and the mist sprayed him, saturating his shirt and pants. Everyone else had donned the slickers provided, but he'd been too concerned, too much in a hurry to find Laurie and Morgan to bother about a raincoat.

He had to make sure they were okay. He couldn't afford to lose anyone else he loved. Loved? What was he thinking? He liked Laurie, liked her a lot. Even Morgan had her moments. But love? He wasn't ready to love again. He might never be. He couldn't ever go through what he'd been through before. He certainly wasn't going to take a chance on losing the ones he loved again.

Everybody on the deck looked alike in their raincoats. Men, women, and children all in yellow slickers, taking pictures, watching the water tumble down the gorge, shouting above the roar of the Falls. The spray doused his hair and matted his eyelashes together, making it even harder to spot the two people he was looking for in the crowd. As it turned out, *they* found him.

"Cooper," Laurie shouted, putting her hand on his wet shoulder. "What are you doing here?"

He whirled around and threw his arms around her while Morgan watched, still perched in her backpack and dressed in a tiny rain slicker with a hood that covered her red-gold baby curls. "You had me worried," he muttered gruffly in Laurie's ear.

"Sorry," she said breathlessly, "but we couldn't tear ourselves away, even for lunch. This is so exciting, being right down here in the middle of it all."

Morgan expressed her agreement by tangling her hands in Cooper's hair and pulling it happily.

"She loves the rainbows," Laurie explained, smiling up at him. "Have you seen them?" She pointed to the spectrum of color created by the mist that hovered just overhead.

Relief coursed through his body, so strong that it made him shake. He found them. They were safe. He dropped his arms to his sides. "I've seen the rainbows," he said. "What I want to see right now is some dry clothes and lunch. Have you eaten?"

Laurie shook her head and he grabbed her hand to walk back along the windy, narrow walkway, passing more visitors who'd come to visit the Cave of the Winds. When Morgan and Laurie had returned their raincoats, and they were all back outside in the pale autumn sunshine, Laurie looked Cooper over.

"You're soaked," she said, noting how his pants stuck to the muscles in his thighs, how his shirt molded to the contours of his broad shoulders and his flat stomach. The man was unbelievably attractive, wet or dry. But he scarcely seemed to know he was soaked to the skin. He was staring at her with such intensity in his eyes that she felt her heart bang against her ribs.

"I see that," he said with a look that said he saw a lot more than that. Then he reached behind her and took the backpack from her, with Morgan still in it. "Come back with me to my room. I'll change and we'll eat. You've got to be hungry, and tired of carrying her around."

Laurie nodded. The cool autumn breeze must be turning Cooper into an iceberg and yes, she *was* tired. She hadn't realized that her shoulders were stiff and she knew Morgan needed something to eat. Maybe they all did. She thought about waiting for him in the lobby, but before she knew it, they were all in the elevator on their way to the third floor, to that luxurious room with the view of the Falls, with Morgan happily riding on Cooper's back, and Laurie carrying her diaper bag.

Once in the room, Cooper handed Morgan to Laurie and disappeared into the bathroom. Laurie changed Morgan's diaper on a waterproof pad, then gave her a bottle of apple juice and a cracker. She tried to ignore the sound of the shower, tried to wipe out images of Cooper standing under the hot water as it coursed down his shoulders and all the way down his naked body to his feet. The image made her feel light-headed, or was it due instead to the lack of food? She hadn't eaten since breakfast and even the mashed peas she offered Morgan from a small jar almost looked good to her at that point.

When Cooper came out of the bathroom wrapped only in a towel around his waist, Laurie jerked her head toward the window and the view of the Falls. Just how much could a woman take of a half-dressed man without losing her cool completely? And this was not just any man. This was Cooper Buckingham, hydraulic engineer, apple picker, favorite of little girls— and big ones, too.

All she could think about was racing across the room to flatten her palms against his bare chest, to feel his heart beat in time with hers. She swallowed hard and stared at her hands clasped tightly in her lap. She was aware that Cooper had opened the built-in dresser drawer and then closed it. She heard him slide open the door to the closet, slide it back into place and then return to the bathroom.

Morgan, full of peas, apple juice and crackers, fell asleep in the middle of the king-size bed. Just like the last time, Laurie thought, which seemed about two years ago. In between she and Cooper had eaten many more meals together, worked together and exchanged a few searing kisses, too.

And now what? What would they do next? Where was it all leading? Nowhere, she told herself firmly. It all came back to her in a flash of crystal clarity. The reason she was there—to take care of Morgan. And the reason *he* was there—to escape involvement by taking only temporary jobs like this one. She wanted love, marriage, kids, the whole nine yards.

He wanted to do his job and then go on to another. To enjoy her company for a short time and then move on to someone else. She was attracted to him, and he was hard to resist. He was kind and considerate and a hard worker besides. But none of that changed a thing.

Laurie smoothed Morgan's damp hair back from her flushed cheek and promised herself she would be strong this time. That she *had* learned something from her past. That she *would* hold out for the right man. But how could a man look and feel any more right than Cooper? She wondered as he walked back into the bedroom dressed in clean khakis and a plaid cotton shirt. His hair was still damp from the shower and her fingers itched to run through it.

"Lunch?" he asked, standing at the foot of the bed, the smell of the European hotel soap wafting her way.

She tried to speak, but suddenly her vocal cords wouldn't work. It might have been just hunger that made everything tighten up inside, or it might have been the half smile on his face. His gaze slid to the baby sleeping in the middle of his bed.

"I see we've lost one of our group."

Laurie nodded, grateful for the distraction Morgan provided.

"Then why don't we order from Room Service?" he suggested.

She nodded again and he picked up the telephone. She scarcely heard what he said. His voice was a low rumble, a soothing sound that promised delicious food to come. When he hung up she finally came to her senses.

"What happened this morning?" she asked. "Did you fix the...uh..."

"Penstock?" he asked with a grin. "Not yet. But I think I can. I just don't know how long it will take me. I have to go back this afternoon. The other guys are probably working on it right now while I'm here. Will you be all right without me?" he asked.

"Of course," she said without hesitation. "When Morgan wakes up we'll go out for a walk."

"You can take one of the stone bridges to Goat Island. But be back here...say at four o'clock."

The food came and the busboy set the tray on the table at the window. Before he left the room the young man lifted the cover on a glass bowl of green leafy salad and two plates of sizzling shrimp scampi with rice.

"It looks wonderful," Laurie said, taking one of the wing chairs at the small round table. "Hotel life sure has its advantages. Especially if you can't cook."

"That's what I always thought," he mused, "until... Well, our friends Steve and Gretel don't have it so bad."

Laurie put her fork down. "If it weren't for the apples." She rubbed the small of her back, still feeling the muscles ache.

"What you need is a back rub," he said softly, watching her.

Laurie pretended not to hear. Instead she concentrated on the food in front of her. She mustn't think of lying flat on the bed, with only a towel to cover her, being massaged by Cooper, his broad hands finding every tender and sensitive spot, his fingers so strong, so skillful, so sure. She felt her face grow warm as tingling sensations radiated through her body. She was spared having to come up with any kind of answer when Cooper looked at his watch, ate the last shrimp on his plate and said goodbye. Reminding her to be back in the lobby at four o'clock, he went back to work.

But when four o'clock came and went and Laurie and Morgan were nowhere to be found, he returned to the hotel room to look for them. When he opened the door he saw Morgan was just where she was when he'd left, flat on her stomach in the middle of the bed. Laurie was sitting in the chair by the window, facing the Falls, reading. He stood in the doorway for a long moment, staring at her. Her pale blond hair brushed against her shoulders. He willed her to turn and smile at him. The smile that made him feel that he could move mountains.

As if she felt his eyes on her, she turned slowly and smiled at him. His heart turned over. Emotions he'd kept buried flooded his mind. The peaceful sleeping baby, the sight of Laurie in the chair, her legs draped over the side, waiting for him when he came home from work. Once that was all he ever wanted from life. He'd almost had it. But it had disappeared in seconds. In one night. One nightmare. It could happen again. He could reach out for happiness and have it all snatched away again. It was better not to try, not to even hope.

He cleared his throat. "What's happening?" he asked her.

She put her book down, stood and stretched like a contented cat, her sweater riding up her midriff showing an expanse of flat stomach. He wanted to cross the room and throw his arms around her. He ached to hold her, to kiss her, to take her sweater off over her head and bury his face between her breasts. To tell her everything he'd been holding back, everything that had happened to him.

But he knew what she'd say. It's over. Put it behind you. Get on with your life. Take another chance. Words that were easy to say, but impossible to do. He couldn't do it. "Morgan never woke up," she explained. "So I let her sleep. It was nice to just sit here and read and look at the view."

As if she was just waiting for Cooper to arrive, Morgan turned over and opened her eyes. Her delighted smile said it all. Cooper was there. It was time to get up and get going. She held out her arms to him, but he held his arms stiffly at his sides. He couldn't pick her up. She wasn't his. His baby was gone.

Laurie shot him a brief puzzled look, then went to the bed and lifted Morgan to her shoulder. Grabbing a clean diaper she took the baby into the bathroom. "Be back in a minute," she said. "Are we leaving?"

"No," he said to her through the bathroom door. "That's the bad news. I can't leave until tomorrow. The good news is I think I fixed it."

When she came out of the bathroom with a clean, fresh-smelling Morgan in her arms, she said, "If you fixed it, why can't we leave?"

He explained as best he could, in layman's terms, how the crack had to withstand a certain pressure over a certain period of time before he could be certain. He saw her look around the room while she was listening, as if just seeing it for the first time, and he knew what she was thinking. Just what he'd been thinking. Where would they all sleep?

"Ready for that walk now?" he asked her.

She hesitated for just a minute and he thought about her sore back. "I'll carry Morgan," he offered. "We'll go over to Goat Island. It's a nice walk. You'll like it. I don't know about you, but I've been in that plant all day and I've got to get out. We apple pickers have got to stay in shape." He tucked a strand of blond hair behind her ear and hoped she didn't guess that he had to get out of that room before he got lost in the depths of her warm hazel eyes, before he lost all desire to leave her or the room until he'd kissed her again.

The night ahead loomed before them, long and full of opportunities and temptations. All of which he had to resist. The wary look in her eyes told him she was just as determined as he was to resist temptation.

They walked briskly across the stone bridge to the island, the mood considerably lighter and impersonal as they escaped the confines of the warm and charmingly seductive bedroom. Morgan was bouncing happily on Cooper's back, and the air was cool and brisk—perfect for walking. Laurie felt a spring in her step. She ought to feel guilty for not picking apples today, but she felt alive and rejuvenated. She'd enjoyed the afternoon, sitting by the window, reading the history of Niagara Falls, and staring out at the magnificent display of rushing water. As Morgan slept, Laurie daydreamed, dreamed that she had everything she wanted, a man who loved her and a baby of her own.

When Cooper came through the door, she thought for one magic moment that it *had* all come true. She had to remind herself sternly that Cooper was *not* the man of her dreams. No matter how much electricity between them, no matter how he looked at her over the kitchen table or across a bedroom with those smoldering eyes, the look that told her he wanted her.

The heat of passion had always been there between them, threatening to explode into a thousand pieces unless she was on guard against it. It mustn't, it shouldn't and it *wouldn't* if she could help it, and she could. She was strong, she was determined and she was not going to give in until she found Mr. Right. Cooper Buckingham was Mr. Wrong. Wrong, wrong wrong, she repeated in time to her steps.

"What was that?" Cooper asked her, striding along beside her.

"What? Oh, nothing," she assured him, squaring her shoulders. She knew that tonight would be the real test, a test she *must* pass. If only Cooper wasn't so relentlessly attractive, so appealing, so generous, so sexy—she sighed. This was not the way to prepare herself mentally for the night ahead, she realized. She should be reciting a list of his faults, not his virtues. But for the life of her she couldn't think of any.

She stole a look at him out of the corner of her eye. He caught her glance and reached for her hand, and they walked together, the three of them. Laurie was conscious of the looks from strangers as they passed, of the smiles they inspired, aware of the picture they made—a tall man, a blond woman and a pink-cheeked baby on the man's back.

They think we're a family, she realized as the warmth from Cooper's fingers warmed her all the way to her heart. But the only one who has a family of her own is Morgan. The rest of us are just playing a role, with no more idea of what it takes to make a marriage and raise a child than the man in the moon. And no more hope, either.

"You're quiet today," Cooper remarked as they passed a cluster of vibrant red maple trees in full fall regalia.

"Just thinking of all the apples I'm not picking," she said with a small guilty smile.

"That's my fault," he said. "I made you come and now we won't get back until tomorrow.

"I wanted to come," she assured him. "I think I needed a break. We all did. I just wonder..." She pulled her hand from his and continued walking, her hand in her pockets.

"Where we're all going to sleep tonight?" he asked.

She was grateful for the cool breeze that fanned her cheeks. "How the work is going back at the farm," she lied. It was only natural they'd both be thinking about the night ahead. But if she pretended it didn't matter who slept where, that it wasn't important enough to worry about, maybe he'd believe her. But from the knowing look in his eyes, she was afraid he didn't.

"I'm sure everything is fine. The workers know what they're doing," Cooper said with a shrug.

Laurie nodded. If only she could be so casual about it. About him. About everything. There was no future in this relationship, so why worry about it? Cooper didn't. She should take a clue from his behavior. If he wasn't worried about all three of them staying in his room, why should she?

After their walk they had dinner in the same dining room where they'd met, then watched television in the lounge without really paying attention. The only thing that lodged in Laurie's brain was the weatherman forecasting possible thunderstorms in upper New York State. But she forgot about the weather when Morgan fell asleep in her arms and they went upstairs to Cooper's room.

He lit a fire in the fireplace, turned off the lights and they sat at the window in matching upholstered chairs watching the lights turn the cascading water into a magical display and sipping an after-dinner brandy.

Laurie knew she was in danger of falling under the spell of the moment. She knew, but suddenly she didn't care. Yes, she'd vowed never to be taken in by another gorgeous man, by a sexy voice or by a heated glance. But Cooper wasn't trying to take her in. He'd been upfront with her from the beginning. There was no hope of this ever turning into anything even vaguely permanent. She knew that, she just didn't know why he felt that way.

Suddenly a flash of lighting lit the sky, more dramatic than any artificial lights, and was followed by a hollow boom of thunder. Laurie gasped and her heart pounded.

Cooper gave her a surprised look. "Don't tell me you're afraid of a little thunder and lightning?" he asked.

"No, of course not." Bravely she raised her glass again then set it down on the floor with a thump. "Well, maybe just a little. But I'm fine now. What . . . were you going to say something?"

"As a matter of fact I was going to propose a toast. To the future."

"Mine or yours?" she asked, looking at him instead of the sky outside.

"Yours wherever it may be."

"I've been thinking of joining the French Foreign Legion," she said jokingly.

He choked on his brandy.

"What's wrong? You don't think I'd have the nerve to do it?"

"I don't think they let women in, but I think you could do anything you put your mind to," he said solemnly. Hah, she thought. She'd put her mind and her heart and her soul to getting married and having a baby and look where it had gotten her. Taking care of somebody else's baby. Falling in love with men who didn't want to get married. Not to her, anyway.

"Let's drink to your future instead," she suggested. "At least you know what's in store for you . . . excitement, adventure taming one of the great rivers of the world."

He didn't look that excited about the prospect, Laurie thought with a glance at his profile in the semidarkness. She only hoped he couldn't read between the lines, couldn't guess that if he asked her she'd follow him from river to river. But she was safe. He wouldn't ask.

Out of the corner of her eye she saw the lightning again, zigzagging across the night sky. She held her breath until she heard the thunder that always followed. Then she started to shake uncontrollably.

Cooper got out of his chair and pulled her up by the shoulders. "You *are* scared, aren't you?" he asked, tightening his hold on her. "Don't be."

"I...I can't help it. It's stupid, I know, but I was on a flight once, a few years ago. Somewhere over Kansas our plane was struck by lightning. It knocked out the plane's electric system. We fell 10,000 feet in half a minute."

"Oh my God," he said.

"That's what I said," she said, brushing a strand of hair off her forehead. "But I didn't panic. The pilot regained control and I soothed the passengers. I acted like it happened every day. We continued to Newark airport and landed safely. Nobody was seriously hurt. Everybody walked off the plane." She looked at Cooper, but her mind was miles and years away. "When I got into the airport, I fell apart. I threw up in the ladies' room. I couldn't sleep for weeks. Every time I fell asleep I'd relive the whole thing, the storm, the lightning, the thunder, and finally the plunge toward the earth. You know how they say the scenes of your life flash in front of you?"

He nodded.

"Well, all I could think of as we fell to our certain death was that I hadn't collected the headsets. Isn't that crazy?" Her voice shook and Cooper pulled her close and wrapped her in his strength, his compassion and his understanding.

Slowly he turned his head until his lips met hers, in a kiss that gave warmth, assurance and asked nothing in return. She tightened her arms around his neck and kissed him back, wanting to forget, wanting to pour out her fears, to lose them forever in his arms. The intensity of their kisses increased. She wanted more from him than comfort, but she couldn't have it. She ought to know that by now. She pulled away, her lips tingling, her whole body aching. She reached for the drink she'd left on the floor and steadied herself with one hand against the back of the chair.

He picked up his glass and raised it. "Here's my favorite toast," he proposed. "May you be in heaven half an hour before the Devil knows you're dead."

"Where did that come from?" she asked with a shaky laugh.

"It's a Scottish toast my grandfather used to say," he said, his eyes warming and kindling a flame somewhere near her heart. Then he took their empty glasses and set them on the table.

He's here, she told herself. We're here together, but not for long. One night, that's all. The baby was sleeping soundly. She might as well relax and enjoy it. But just as she'd willed herself to relax, another flash of lightning shot through the sky and lit the room. It was closer and brighter than the one before and was followed immediately by a loud booming roar of thunder.

Laurie threw her arms around Cooper and he gathered her in, kissing her frantically, her eyelids, her temples, her lips, seeking...giving comfort. The lights flickered and went out. Cooper lifted Laurie off the floor, staggered across the floor in the dark and set her on top of the waist-high chest of drawers.

"I want you, Laurie," he muttered against her mouth. "Whenever I'm with you I want you so desperately. And when I'm not with you I can't stop thinking about you. Why is that?"

Her answer was to lean forward, put her arms around his neck and kiss him eagerly, passionately, wildly while the weather outside the picture window grew as wild as their passion.

A roaring heat flared between them. Laurie's lips parted and he delved into her mouth with his tongue, seeking, exploring, mating with hers in the most elemental way. All rational thought was gone, replaced by a frantic need, a compulsion to make her his, to take her there and then. She wrapped her legs around him to bring him closer and he felt his control slipping away. He pressed her against his chest, against his arousal until he couldn't breathe, couldn't think.

She made tiny noises in the back of her throat that urged him on. She was so responsive, so warm, so open, so giving. Possessed by a hunger to feel her warm skin, he slipped his hands under her shirt and cupped her breasts in his hands, massaging the tender buds, feeling them harden with need under his touch.

"Please, Cooper," she whispered against his lips. "Please..." He cut off her words with a hot, searing kiss that left her throbbing with desire. She was only vaguely aware she was on a chest of drawers. All she knew was that she wanted Cooper, wanted him then and there. Wanted to be part of him, part of his body, part of his life. If only he'd let her, she could make him alive again, fully, completely. She could, she knew she could. If he'd let her.

Without breaking the kiss he lifted her from the chest. She tightened her legs around him, clinging to him, not knowing or caring where they were going. The world spun around her, her incoherent thoughts revolving around this man, and his strength, his masculinity, his desire. He wanted her. The certainty of that made her spirits soar. He wanted her. She wanted him. What could be more simple?

The bedroom was dark. The whole hotel was dark. The baby slept. The rain beat against the window as he took her down on the thick, plush carpet and leaned over her. "Laurie," he said.

The word was a question, and she answered it by reaching for him, pulling him down on top of her. The heat from his body made her dizzy. Her mind said yes, but the word stuck in her throat.

If she couldn't tell him, she had to show him how she felt. She ran her hands through his hair, thick and dark and heavy. She pulled him closer and kissed him until he moaned deep in his throat.

"Do you know what you're doing to me?" he demanded, his hands on her shoulders, his lips a breath away from her.

She shook her head. She wanted him to tell her, to show her.

He paused and brushed her lips with his. "Yes, you do," he muttered, his warm breath teasing and tantalizing her warm skin.

Her hands grew restless. She wanted to touch his skin, to feel the muscles in his thighs, the hard planes of his chest. She reached under his shirt as he'd reached under hers a minute ago. She ran her hands over the crisp dark hair on his chest, reveling in the feel of him. She heard him gasp when she reached the waistband of his slacks and he breathed harder, faster.

Lightning illuminated the room once again, lasting only long enough for her to see his face above her, to see the passion burning in his eyes. The thunder rocked the floor beneath them, or was that her imagination? She clung to him, pressed her lips against his throat and tried to kick off her pants at the same time. She didn't know how she could exist if he didn't fill the emptiness inside her. Now. This minute.

He was busy yanking off his slacks before helping her with hers. He turned her on her side to face him, the carpet soft and warm beneath them, and tugged her sweater off over her head. He tossed it to one side and then there was nothing between them but her panties and his briefs. Her breasts were full and warm and heavy in his hands. He heard her short, quick intake of breath as he buried his face in their lush fullness.

With one hand he covered her flat stomach and reached lower with sure, knowing fingers.

"Yes," she breathed. "Oh, yes." And she arched her body to meet his. If he stopped now she'd surely die. Did he know that?

Somewhere in the distance a telephone was ringing, nagging and insistent. Only it wasn't really in the distance. It was right there in the room. Ringing so loudly she was afraid Morgan would wake up. She paused only a moment, just in time to look at Cooper and to realize the mood was broken. With a groan, Laurie got to her feet and grabbed the receiver.

"I'm very sorry," said a clipped polite voice, "about the power outage. I hope it hasn't caused any inconvenience."

"Inconvenience? No, not at all," she said shakily, running a hand through her tousled hair.

"We expect to have everything in order before morning," the concierge assured her.

Laurie hung up. She looked around the room, still dazed and confused. Everything would be in order by morning; it would take longer than that for her to still her beating heart, to even look Cooper square in the eyes. She was vaguely aware he was dressing and she wasn't. She grabbed her clothes from the floor and went to the bathroom to shower and dress.

When she came back he was standing at the window staring into the darkness. She didn't know what to say, so she did nothing. There was something about his stance and his silence that confirmed her feeling that the moment was over. The passion that had flared so brightly had been extinguished by the ring of the phone.

She felt cold and alone even though there were three of them in the room. She got into bed and stared at Cooper's back, wondering what he was thinking.

"I didn't mean for that to happen," he said in the darkness.

"I know you didn't. At least admit you *wanted* it to happen," she said. He didn't say anything. She turned her head and shivered. "All right, *I* was the one who wanted it. But it doesn't work that way, does it? It doesn't work unless both people feel the same about each other. You'd think I would have learned that by now, but I haven't." Her voice caught and the tears threatened again.

He opened his mouth to speak, to protest, but she wouldn't let him. She had to let it all out now. To make sure he knew how she felt. "Believe me, I won't make the same mistake again. The next time I fall in love it will be with someone who's free, who doesn't come with any emotional baggage, who..." She faltered and she couldn't continue, not with her throat choked with tears.

Cooper's brow furrowed. His lips parted, the lines deepened in his forehead. "What did you say?"

"I said I won't make the same mistake again."

"No, about falling in love. You're not in love with me, are you?"

She swallowed hard. "Of course not."

"And if you were?" he asked in a voice so low she almost didn't hear him.

"If I were...if I were..." If she were she'd cry herself to sleep, pound the wall in frustration, stomp on the floor, anything but stand there discussing it rationally with the man she'd come this close to making love with, who was looking at her so intensely, who was half dressed, his rumpled shirt only partly covering his chest.

Facing him like this was more than she could bear, after what they'd done here tonight and what they hadn't done. Her body still ached with frustration, her skin felt so sensitive and vulnerable. Her fingertips longed to touch him again, to feel his body respond to her touch. She wanted to hear his voice in the heat of passion call her name. She turned over and buried her face in the pillow, wishing she'd never come back to Niagara Falls. Hoping she'd learn her lesson at last.

Cooper stood there watching her sleep and listening to the wind howl outside the window, feeling unfulfilled and hollow inside. The frustration built up as he turned over the scene in his mind. Laurie, the most generous, warmhearted woman in the world had offered herself to him, even knowing how he felt, knowing there was no future for them.

He'd almost taken her up on it. If it hadn't been for the telephone, where would they be now? Lying on the carpet, sated, fulfilled, satisfied beyond his wildest dreams? He had no doubt of that. His arms would be around her all night long. His body burned, throbbed with frustration.

Did she love him? She might think she did, but that was his fault. He had to make it clear to her that he wasn't free to love again. Instead he encouraged her, he kissed her, he wanted her, he took what she offered and gave her nothing in return. He had nothing to give.

There was more. He felt admiration and affection for her. He wanted to tell her he'd give anything if he were free to love again, to take another chance on love and start a new life. If he'd met her sooner. But that wasn't how life worked. He couldn't choose the time or place or the person.

Laurie was the right person. She was strong, she was sweet, she was everything a man could want. She could comfort hundreds of passengers in the middle of a disaster and yet fall apart in a thunderstorm in his arms. He sighed loudly and lay down on the far side of the bed next to Morgan. When he finally put his tortured body and his tormented mind to rest it was almost dawn.

Chapter Seven

Cooper got the good news in the morning that his repair job was a success. The patch worked, the water stopped leaking and there was no reason for him to hang around. His boss told him to enjoy his "vacation."

Morgan, Laurie and Cooper had breakfast in the coffee shop of the hotel before they headed back to the orchard. Cooper left an extra large tip he hoped would make up for the pile of crumbs Morgan scattered under her high chair from her bran muffin. He tried to apologize to the waitress, but she waved it aside, saying she had one of her own at home, about the same age. He didn't even try to explain that Morgan wasn't theirs.

But he wondered, as he surveyed Morgan sitting at the table in her pink coveralls, if the waitress's baby could possibly be as cute as Morgan. She didn't cry as much as she had when he first met her, he noticed. She was usually happy, as long she got what she wanted. He occasionally held her in his arms, just for a moment while Laurie was busy, but never long enough to get attached to her or to feel any emotional tie.

He realized, as they drove through the fertile fields dotted with fruit trees, that he was looking forward to going back. He almost thought "back home," but stopped himself. It wasn't his home. He didn't have a home. And he wasn't going to get bogged down thinking of what might have been.

Laurie's voice broke into his reverie. "We're not taking you away too soon, are we? What if there's another crack?"

"I left the number. If they need me, they'll call," he assured her.

"I didn't realize how important your job was until I read that book about the Falls yesterday. About how much power is produced and how much money is involved. I read how they draw extra water during the night and store it in reservoirs so the flow over the Falls won't be diminished during the day. I was thinking about that last night."

"I thought you were asleep," he said, keeping his eyes on the road. He'd envied her and Morgan's sound sleep while he chased the shadows from his mind, willing the memories of the past to fade and recede.

"I was," she said, turning toward him. "But what about you? Did we leave you enough room?"

Room? They'd left him too much room and too much time. The darkened room, the ready-made family asleep in his bed. As much as he enjoyed their company, was looking forward to returning to the farm, he had to break it off. And soon. Being with the two of them, Laurie and Morgan, acting like a family, had brought it all back, and with it the pain. He ought to drop them at the doorstep and sign up for another temporary job. But there were those damnable apples. His commitment to Steve, and sweet little Morgan, who for some unknown reason, had taken a liking to him. And finally there was Laurie, who was proving more and more difficult to treat as a mere friend. Especially after last night. But it had to be done. Soon, before he made love to her one of these dark and stormy nights, or a clear day, or...

"Plenty of room," he assured her a little belatedly. But she looked at him as if she wasn't sure about that. He hoped she didn't know he'd paced the floor most of the night before he fell into bed next to Morgan. He hoped Laurie hadn't seen him reach out and touch the baby's soft cheek, then hastily withdraw his hand. He didn't want her to know that the baby's sweet scent had caused a shaft of pain to pierce his heart. But how could she?

When they got back to the house Laurie changed into dirt-stained jeans and a baggy sweatshirt. Cooper set up the playpen under the trees hoping to keep Morgan happy for a while so they could both pick. Then they went up the ladders, each with a canvas bag over their shoulders. Morgan rattled a plastic tetrahedron educational toy with varied plastic shapes inside it and Laurie held her breath, hoping they'd get a few boxes filled before Morgan lost interest and demanded to be released from behind the bars of her playpen.

"Does that kind of thing happen very often?" Cooper asked, looking down at the baby.

"What?" she asked from behind the tree. "That I sleep with strangers in their hotel rooms? No, no matter what wild rumors you've heard about us, flight attendants usually lead very dull lives."

Copper grinned at her between the branches, a flash of even white teeth in his suntanned face. "I'm relieved to hear it. But no, I didn't mean that. I meant, are most kids Morgan's age able to distinguish shapes the way she can? Look at her," he said, gesturing in the direction of the playpen as Morgan fit the round piece into the round hole.

Laurie paused with an apple in her hand and gazed at Morgan. "She's pretty remarkable, isn't she?" she said softly. "But then so is her mother."

"Steve is no slouch either," he said, continuing to fill his canvas sack with apples. "He was Phi Beta Kappa plus the star of the soccer team."

"So she comes by it naturally," Laurie murmured, "her intelligence and her coordination."

"What about you?" Cooper asked. "I'll bet you never lose your cool."

"Me? When I was a flight attendant, I was scared to death in turbulence, ever since . . . you know. I do what I'm supposed to do, but the smile is one that's pasted on my face. Underneath I'm a bowl of jello."

He appeared to be studying her for signs of quivering, so Laurie planted her feet firmly on the top rung of the ladder to show him that was then and this was now and launched into another flight attendant story.

"I'll never forget the time I got stuck in Kansas City just before my sister's wedding," she began, and then went on to describe the route she'd finally taken, through Phoenix and Salt Lake City. Cooper seemed amused especially when she came to the part about leaving her suitcase in the overhead compartment after repeating hundreds of times not to do that very thing. She ended up having to borrow a dress from her sister to be her bridesmaid.

When Cooper laughed out loud Laurie realized she didn't care how flaky she seemed if it got a laugh out of him.

"You and your sister are close," he remarked, looking at her with something like envy in his expression.

"Very," she said, "though you wouldn't believe it to hear us rag on each other." She paused for a moment and studied the apple in her hand. "She's going to have a baby soon."

"That'll be nice for you," he remarked, "to have a niece or nephew."

She nodded, but her lower lip trembled.

"But you want one of your own," he said quietly.

"Yes. No. I don't need one of my own," she said a little too fervently. "I'll have a niece or nephew to spoil whenever I want to. And Morgan here." She sent a reassuring smile in Cooper's direction.

He glanced at Morgan in her playpen, engrossed in pounding on her toy piano, filling the air with discordant sounds. Laurie and Cooper exchanged a long look of mutual understanding bordering on pride. Why? She wasn't theirs. But they'd accomplished something just by keeping her happy. Laurie tore her gaze from Cooper when she heard the sound of an approaching car above the banging of the toy piano. There across the field she saw a car pull up on the road next to the fence. She backed down the ladder, and tossed her sack onto the ground.

"Who's that?" Cooper asked, following her down the ladder.

She shook her head and they walked briskly together toward the fence where four people, a man, woman and two children had gotten out of the car and were waving and calling to them.

"Hello," the man yelled.

"A case of mistaken identity," Laurie said to Cooper. "That's all. Hi," she called when they were close enough to see the out-of-state licence plate on their car. "Can we help you?"

"The woman at the country store at the crossroads told us you had a roadside stand where we could buy fresh produce."

Laurie exchanged a quick glance with Cooper, "Sorry," she said. "But it sounds like a good idea. Maybe we ought to try it. But this is just an ordinary orchard."

They nodded, piled back in their car and took off.

At that moment Morgan let out a loud scream and Laurie ran back to get her. She lifted her out of the playpen and gave her a snack of a banana and a cup of juice. Then she peeled a banana for herself and sat down under the tree with Morgan in her lap wondering what was taking Cooper so long.

When he finally appeared from the opposite direction they'd come from, she looked up inquiringly. "I ran into one of the farm workers," he said, holding out a half-eaten apple in his hands. "Look what they found."

Laurie wrinkled her nose. "Who did that?"

He shook his head. "They said it looks like deer. They've stripped the branches on a dozen or more trees out on the back forty where the workers are."

"Deer, as in Bambi? How could a sweet little deer do all that damage? It must have been a whole herd. What do we do about it?"

"They said when there are more workers, they stand guard at night."

"And then what, shoo them away?"

He shrugged. "I guess."

Laurie tried to rise to her feet, but with Morgan falling asleep in her arms, she gratefully accepted Cooper's outstretched hand. To her surprise, he took Morgan out of her arms and they walked back to the house together as if they'd decided they'd had it for the day. Laurie's mind was spinning with the possibility of a roadside stand, of deer decimating the crop but most of all with the image of Morgan's face cradled against Cooper's shoulder. In the nursery, Cooper put Morgan into her crib and covered her with her blanket while Laurie watched.

Laurie tried to act nonchalant, as if it happened every day, Cooper putting Morgan to bed, but it didn't and she didn't want to say anything that would embarrass him. But watching Morgan's eyelashes flutter as she snuggled under the blanket caused a longing so fierce to fill her heart that she pressed her hand against her chest. Cooper's gaze met hers and she thought she saw a longing that matched her own. But for what? For a baby? He said not. For her?

A shiver went up her spine. With a jolt Laurie was taken back to the first night they'd come here together, when they'd stood this way looking down at a sleeping Morgan, when the breeze had blown through the curtains as it did now, bringing with it the sweet scent of ripening apples, bringing, too, a heightened awareness of each other, a tingling of the senses, an excitement that surged through them, a longing that couldn't be denied today any more than last night. Feeling the touch of his hands on her shoulders, she turned to face him and lift her lips to his, just as she'd done that last time in the nursery.

But this time it happened, as she'd wanted it to before. In spite of what happened last night, or maybe because of it, his kiss was instantly searing, demanding, possessive, promising nothing, asking nothing in return. He knew better than to do that. But she gave him everything she had, all the pent-up emotion of the last few days. All the frustration of sharing that bed with him last night, but sleeping on opposite sides, of the phone call that pulled them apart. The frustration of sharing this house and this baby came out in their wild kisses, their frantic desire to close the gap between them. Laurie staggered backward, her heart pounding wildly, and reached for the wall with the back of her hand so she wouldn't fall down.

"What was that..." She choked, unable to finish her sentence.

"Just a kiss," he said with a half smile that sent her heartbeat off the chart again. But his pounding pulse, as he gripped the side of the crib for support, told Cooper it was more than just a kiss.

He had no business kissing Laurie like that, like he meant it, like he couldn't get enough of her. Not now or ever. It wasn't fair of him to lead her on. And it wasn't fair for her to look at him the way she was doing now, as if she knew something about him he didn't know about himself. What that was didn't bear thinking about. It was time to apologize and get out of this room, this room that had a very strange effect on him.

"Sorry about that," he muttered.

"Why?" she asked, leaning against the wall and staring at him.

"You know why," he said, locking his gaze with hers. "You deserve better. Somebody who's got something to offer you."

"What about—"

"I told you before. I was married once and that was it. I'm not going to get married again and I'm not having children again." He didn't mean to say "again." He hoped she hadn't noticed. The look in her eyes, those wide expressive eyes that mirrored her feelings, told him she did. But in the long silence that followed, he realized she wasn't going to pursue the subject. Not now anyway, and he would make sure there was no opportunity to pursue it any other time.

"All right. Where were we?" she asked, looking around the room.

He couldn't help it. He wanted to answer her question by taking up where they'd left off, by pulling her to him again, to taste her sweetness, to feel her body mold to his and lose himself in the sensations that swept through his body. But he couldn't and he wouldn't. He clenched his fists at his sides, squared his shoulders and reminded her they had a problem with deer.

Laurie blinked rapidly to hide her disappointment, but he saw it and he felt terrible. But what could he do? He shouldn't be there at all. If he felt an obligation to Steve, then he should pick apples and leave it at that. He couldn't seem to do that. Carrying the baby in his arms, putting her to bed left him feeling shaken and aware. Aware of Laurie, aware of how it could be, of how it should be, if only... Aware of how she looked and how she felt in his arms.

Before he could say anything else, Laurie turned on her heel and left the nursery.

Chapter Eight

Cooper woke up early the next morning to the sound of rain on the roof. He peered out the window at the steady drops that fell and then dressed quickly to see what condition the orchard was in. Funny how concerned he'd become, how much a part of life on a farm he felt in such a short time. No, it wasn't a bad life, he thought, stuffing his arms into the sleeves of his jacket and walking quietly down the hall. He paused at the door of Morgan's room. She was sleeping soundly on her back, her arms flung straight out like a red-haired angel. Temperamentally, she was far from angelic, but right now.... He smiled and continued to Gretel and Steve's master bedroom.

He knocked softly on the door, but Laurie didn't answer. He didn't want to wake her. She needed her rest after picking apples and hauling Morgan around, but if she was awake . . . and if she did want to take a tour of the place, he wouldn't mind the company.

He, the biggest loner around, looking for company on a rainy morning. He shook his head in dismay at what had happened to him. Without his even realizing, and definitely without his permission, he'd gotten used to her company. Sizzling sexual attraction aside, he liked being with her, teasing her, seeing her smile.

He opened the door very softly, just in case . . . But she was fast asleep, her golden hair spread across the pillow, her pale cheek resting on one hand. He stood there for a long moment watching her sleep alone in that huge bed that was meant for two, for two people who made love at night, who slept in each other's arms, who woke up knowing each day would be as good as the day before, maybe even better. He gripped the doorknob tightly and closed the door behind him.

Outside the rain was falling steadily. With his hands jammed in his pockets he walked between rows of apple trees, the damp fragrant earth filling his senses. He had wondered over the years what made Steve buy an apple orchard, but even on a rainy fall day like this, he knew the answer. The feeling of peace and harmony with the earth, with the whole world in fact, filled his heart. Combine that with raising children and hard work and you had a pretty good life for yourself.

Not that he was envious. Steve deserved everything he had. And Cooper had everything he wanted in a job. Excitement, variety and success. So everybody was happy. Then why did he feel a sense of longing, a yearning here in the middle of Steve's orchard?

Footsteps and the snap of a twig underfoot made him turn around. Laurie was walking toward him in a bright red vinyl rain-jacket.

"Nice day," she said as she approached, holding her palm up to catch the raindrops.

"For ducks," he remarked, "but not for apple pickers."

"You're up early," she noted.

He tucked her hair inside the hood of her jacket, wanting nothing more than to kiss the raindrops off her eyelashes, off her cheeks and lips. "Yep. I checked on you and Morgan to see if you wanted to come out with me, but you were both in dreamland."

"You saw me sleeping?" she asked, gazing up at him through wet lashes.

"Just for a minute." But long enough to wish he had an excuse to join her under those blankets, to kiss her awake, to watch the desire grow in her eyes . . .

"I *was* dreaming," she said.

"About me?" he teased.

"How did you know?"

"That satisfied smile on your face."

"I suppose a lot of women dream about you. After all, it's not your fault you're so all-fired attractive," she said with a smile tilting the corner of her mouth. Damned if he wasn't so all-fired attractive, she thought, even with the rain soaking his hair and his skin. It wouldn't surprise her if she dreamed about him every night. But somehow dreams weren't enough. Not anymore.

She was ready for real-life love, a day-and-night love, a forever-after love.

She might have stood there all day staring at him if the rain hadn't started coming down in earnest, blowing the branches of the trees and knocking apples to the ground. With a brief glance at the darkening sky, they ran together back to the house.

After changing into dry clothes, bathing and dressing Morgan, she brought the baby into the kitchen and put her in her high chair. Then she sank down into a kitchen chair and looked across the room at Cooper, now dry and better-looking than ever, if that was possible.

"I don't know about you," she said, "but I feel a little strange today."

He nodded and looked up from a box of pancake mix. "It's called hunger."

"It's more than that. I ache all over. I hate to say it, but I'm not sorry it's too rainy to pick today." She yawned. "I feel like I've already done a day's work."

He reached into the refrigerator for a carton of milk. "You looked like you were sleeping soundly."

"Yes, even though I'm sleeping somewhere different every night."

"You were a flight attendant. You should be used to that."

"I'm used to hotels but despite what you think, we didn't sleep with men we hardly knew."

He set milk on the table. "Do you really hardly know me, Laurie?"

"Well, it hasn't been very long," she said, burying her face in Morgan's red curls. She would not get caught again in that blatant sexy gaze of Cooper's. He had the power to turn her steel resolve into mush, her best intentions into wisps of smoke. She sniffed the air. Smoke. Cooper had turned the heat on under the frying pan, but so far had neglected to make the batter for the pancakes.

"You need some help," she decided, placing Morgan's cereal bowl in front of her.

While Cooper turned off the stove Laurie sat down and read the instructions from the back of the box. But her mind wasn't on pancakes. "I know you, but I can't possibly know you because we just met. That's why it's so strange," she explained under her breath.

An hour later after breaking a few eggs and stirring a lumpy batter, they had a stack of pancakes ready to eat. And just in the nick of time. Laurie's stomach was grumbling in protest.

"This is good," she proclaimed, sharing her pancake with Morgan. "Maybe you were right. It *was* hunger."

He nodded. "I told you so."

"I wish I knew how to cook," she said wistfully.

"So do I."

She set her fork down. "Wish I knew how to cook, or wish *you* did?"

"Both. It's harder than it looks."

She nodded. "Amen." She paused, then took a deep breath. "Was your wife a good cook?"

He froze. Cooper was not in the mood to discuss the past. Especially his past. He set his fork down. "As a matter of fact, yes. Why?"

"I just wondered. Did she...is she... Never mind." She turned to look at Morgan.

Laurie looked so uncertain, so hesitant, so uncomfortable Cooper's heart went out to her. He should have told her before. Should have put all his cards on the table the way she'd done. Then there wouldn't be all these false hopes, unrealistic dreams. Not for him or for her.

"My wife died," he said. And once it was out he was relieved.

"I'm sorry," Laurie murmured.

"It was two years ago," he said. And then the words tumbled out. He hadn't planned on telling her, but once he'd started he couldn't seem to stop.

"She was four months pregnant. It was raining, sleeting in fact. She shouldn't have gone out, but she did. Her car skidded and flipped over. They were both killed instantly. Her and the baby."

The only sound in the room was the grandfather clock in Gretel's living room chiming forlornly. Even Morgan was subdued by the tone of Cooper's voice. He could have stopped there, but he hadn't finished the story, and until he did, it would go round and round in his brain forever. "I wasn't there or I would have taken her. And it never would have happened. I'll never forgive myself."

Laurie reached out to touch him, but suddenly he had to get out of there, to go somewhere where he could let it go. This room just wasn't big enough. He grabbed his jacket from the hook on the wall and strode out once again into the healing, cleansing rain.

Laurie went to the window and stared after him. She couldn't imagine anything worse than losing someone she loved. No wonder Cooper didn't want to try again.

No wonder sadness welled up in his eyes when he thought she wasn't looking. No wonder he didn't want to get attached to Morgan who was so attached to him. She stood in the middle of the kitchen feeling the tears well up in her eyes and spill down her cheeks as the rain streaked the windows.

Only Morgan's insistent cries brought her back to the present. She scooped her up from the high chair and plunked her into her playpen in the middle of the kitchen floor. She didn't want to be alone right now and she was sure Morgan felt the same. She tried to imagine how she'd feel if she were Cooper, two years after a tragedy had happened. Then she made herself think of something else, anything or she'd dissolve into unbearable sadness.

With all the energy she could muster she washed the breakfast dishes and then took one of Gretel's cookbooks from the shelf. It was called, appropriately enough, *The Complete Apple Cookbook*. "Apples, what else?" Laurie mumbled to herself.

"What do you think, Morgan?" she inquired, leafing through the pages. "Apple coffee cake, apple muffins, apple crisp? Not that I'm capable of making any of these, but I can try. After all, your mother was a flight attendant just like me, with all her meals coming on a tray or out of a restaurant kitchen. She learned to cook, so why can't I?"

Morgan didn't answer. She just peered through the slats of her playpen, her head tilted to one side.

While she assembled the ingredients for apple bar cake Laurie couldn't help thinking of Cooper. Wondering where he was, how he was. How he must have suffered. As she measured the flour she imagined the squeal of brakes, the crunch of metal against metal. Wondering how he found out. Did a policeman come to the door or was it a phone call out of the blue? Forcing her attention back to the job at hand, she peeled apples with single-minded determination. Until she heard the back door open.

She wheeled around. Cooper was standing in the doorway, his jacket soaking wet, a grim smile on his face. She heaved a huge sigh of relief at the welcome sight of his wet face and the water running down the sides of his arms. She wanted so badly to hug him to her, rainwater and all, to hold him tightly, to ease his pain.

But she couldn't do that. He didn't want her sympathy. He'd made that quite clear. So she knotted her fingers together. She wouldn't let anything show, but she couldn't help the feelings.

"Where were you?" she asked lightly.

"Picking apples."

"In the rain?"

He nodded, shaking water off his head. "What are you doing?"

She gave the batter a stir, dumped the apples into it and poured it into the cake pan. "Making a cake. But don't get your hopes up. It's my first attempt." She opened the oven door and slid the pan in. "I figured if you can make pancakes, I can make a coffee cake."

The expression in his eyes was unreadable. She wanted to believe things were back to normal. But what was normal? Certainly not this charade of playing house. In any case she had learned something this morning. She'd learned why Cooper was unavailable.

Now she understood why she couldn't fall in love with him, couldn't even get close to him, unless she wanted to give up her dream of marriage and children. And she didn't. It had to stop now, this falling for the wrong person. She sat on the kitchen stool looking out at the rain, scarcely aware that Cooper had gone to change out of his wet clothes. When the oven timer went off she gingerly opened the oven door.

A wonderful smell of brown sugar and cinnamon came wafting into the room. Could it be? Could she have made something edible on her first try?

"Smells good," Cooper said over her shoulder. She hadn't heard him come in. "I thought you said you couldn't—"

"I can't. But I had to try." She lifted the cake from the oven, set it on the counter and cut two pieces. Cooper poured two cups of leftover breakfast coffee and set them on the table. They sat across from each other without speaking, without eating, just looking off into space, anywhere but at each other.

After an eternity she wrapped her hands around her coffee cup and said, "I had no business asking about your past."

He reached for her other hand and held it tightly. "It's okay," he said gruffly. "I should have told you before. You've been up-front with me. But it's not something I wanted to talk about, or even think about."

"I know, I know," she stammered, gripping his fingers. "You would have made a wonderful father."

"Maybe, who knows?" Cooper asked, trying to keep his voice steady. He thought he'd done all his crying two years ago. But this morning, in the orchard, he'd let the tears fall shamelessly, let them mix with the rain as he picked apples and carefully laid them in rows in a box. He was grateful for the repetitious, mindless work. Whether he'd been aware of it or not, it was time to let it all hang out. Get it out of his system. Hopefully for the last time.

He would stop wishing for what might have been. He would come to grips with what was. With what must be. And that was a solitary life. He managed to give her a half smile. "Maybe I'll follow your example. Enjoy other people's kids."

"Do you know anybody with kids?" she asked, pulling her hand away and taking her cup to the stove for something else to do.

"Just Steve." He was just as glad he wasn't anybody's uncle or even godfather. Morgan was as far as he could go.

Laurie wiped her hands on a towel and looked out the window. "I'm going to give Morgan a nap, then I'm going out to do some work in the orchard."

Cooper gave Laurie a long, appraising look. He knew what it was like to be restless. Too restless to stay inside, to talk about feelings, about the past and think about the future. The trees called, the work, the picking and packing soothed the nerves. Laurie was trying to forget, too, trying not to think of a lost opportunity, a personal failure, of what might have been. Maybe that was why he understood her.

While Morgan napped, they worked together under a gentle rain, without speaking, in companionable silence. He hoped she wasn't feeling sorry for him. For the past two years he'd avoided pity by never confiding in anyone. Then along came Laurie and he'd told her everything. He didn't understand it. Didn't understand his feelings for this woman.

He knew he wanted her with a fierce hunger even as she stood on a ladder in the rain, her hair hanging in wet strands from under her rain hat as she gently cupped, lifted and twisted each apple. He wanted to run with her through the rain to the house and strip off every inch of clothing and cover her body with his, warming, teasing, kissing, exploring... To lose himself in her warm, welcoming depths as they shared the ultimate intimacy. He wanted to bury himself in her, to find solace in her arms.

He reached for the tree trunk to brace himself. Enough, he told himself. But it was not enough to think about it, he wanted to do it. And yet he couldn't. It wouldn't be fair to Laurie. He climbed down the ladder. "I'll go check on Morgan," he offered. He had to get away from Laurie, from the haunting expression in her warm hazel eyes, from her enticing curved body partly hidden by her rain jacket.

She looked up briefly, nodded and went back to work. He envied her concentration. His was gone. He couldn't think of apples. He could only think of Laurie. As if their conversation this morning, as painful as it was, had given him permission to fantasize about what would happen if he were free of his past, of his memories. But he wasn't.

Morgan's cries greeted him as he opened the back door. He had a strange feeling of déjà vu. Was it only last week that he'd gone to get her from her nap, changed her diaper for the first time and carried her out to Laurie in the orchard? He didn't want to get attached to this baby. She had a way of reminding him of what he'd lost. But here she was, wide-awake, crying for something. A clean diaper, a drink... some company?

Her face was bright red, her screaming grew louder.

"Morgan," he said, alarmed by her appearance. "What's wrong?"

Usually she stopped crying when she saw him, but not today. Today she screamed even louder, her eyes red-rimmed and glazed with tears. He picked her up. She needed him. Now. He pressed his face to hers, feeling the heat radiate from her cheek to his. She was warm. Too warm. She gulped and whimpered pitifully.

Cooper felt his heart was being squeezed in an apple press. She looked so miserable. He felt so helpless. She was breathing unevenly, crying nonstop. He walked into the living room, holding the fleece-clad baby to his chest, feeling anxious, frustrated and worried. Where was Laurie, why didn't she come in and tell him what to do? Morgan was burning up.

He carried Morgan into the bathroom. With one hand he opened the medicine chest and pawed through it until he discovered what he was looking for—a rectal thermometer. He couldn't do anything with it. Not by himself. He put Morgan back into bed and was about to run out to get Laurie when she came through the door.

"I was wondering what was taking you so long," Laurie said, taking off her rain slicker and boots.

"It's Morgan," he said, gripping Laurie by the arms. "She's burning up with a fever. I can't make her stop crying."

Laurie's eyes widened with fear and they raced back to Morgan's room.

Morgan was lying on her back waving her arms frantically. Laurie picked her up and pressed the back of her hand to the baby's cheek. "You're right," she agreed. "We've got to take her temperature."

He nodded and showed her the thermometer. She read the instructions then shot him a desperate look.

"I'll hold her if you do it," he offered.

Laurie nodded, her eyes suspiciously bright.

"You're not going to cry, too, are you?" he asked.

"Of course not, but I've never done this before," she confessed.

"Me, either."

Somehow they did it, despite Morgan's cries, and read the temperature.

"It's 104 degrees," Laurie said, alarmed.

Morgan was back in her arms, thumb in her mouth, still sniffling, still unhappy.

"We've got to call the doctor," Laurie said.

In the kitchen, pinned to a bulletin board, was a list of phone numbers Gretel had left for her. The pediatrician's was at the top of the list.

"Is she limp and lethargic?" the doctor asked when Laurie reached him.

"No, she's kicking and screaming," Laurie explained over Morgan's cries.

"That's a good sign. Is she eating and drinking?"

Cooper took Morgan out of Laurie's arms and went to the refrigerator for a glass of orange juice. Morgan drank it thirstily. Laurie reached for a pad of paper to write the doctor's orders.

When Laurie hung up she sat on the stool by the phone and sighed heavily. "He thinks it's just a cold."

"Some cold," Cooper said as Morgan pressed her damp forehead against the front of his shirt. His clothes were slowly drying, but they were stuck damply to his body. He felt cold and clammy.

Laurie held out her arms. "I'll take her. You change."

He shook his head and leaned against the refrigerator. "If I move her she might start crying again."

Laurie frowned at the two of them. "Well, sit down, anyway," she said. They moved into the living room and he sat down on the chintz-covered couch, as carefully as he could so as not to disturb the suddenly very tired baby. Cooper leaned back into the cushions and closed his eyes. Morgan's face was nestled against his shoulder. She took several deep, shaky breaths and then shuddered and fell asleep. He exhaled slowly.

Laurie stood in the middle of the room watching them. "I don't know what I would have done if I'd been alone with her," she said, gnawing on her fingernail.

Cooper lifted his head and looked at her with half-closed eyes. "You would have done just fine," he assured her.

"I hope you don't catch her cold," she said.

"That's the least of our problems." Did he say *our* problems? Since when did Laurie's problems become his? Since the first moment he'd seen her. Since the first time he'd heard Morgan cry. Since the first time he'd had lunch with them in the hotel dining room. Since the time Laurie and Morgan came to his room and he drove them home. That was how long her problems had been his. It seemed like forever.

"Let's try to get her to bed," Laurie whispered. "You must be miserable."

Miserable? He was uncomfortably damp, worried about Morgan, but with this little girl finally asleep on his shoulder, and out of *her* misery, he felt a strange kind of peace come over him. No, he wasn't miserable. He was something else. Something he couldn't put a name to. He stood up, slowly so as not to disturb Morgan, and with Laurie following, he walked down the hall and put her in her crib.

Laurie put the palm of her hand against his chest and the warmth from her hand filled his heart. "Thanks," she whispered.

Cooper pressed his lips together in a tight line, his emotions too near the surface to speak. He couldn't help thinking what it would have been like if things had been different, if there'd been no tragedy in his life. He'd missed his one chance for happiness, for a full and happy life. Suddenly the unfairness, the randomness of his wife's accident hit him with the force of a flash flood, roaring through a dry gully. That was him, a dried-up riverbank, growing older by the minute watching life and love pass him by. He turned and went to the guest room to change his clothes.

When he came back to the living room Laurie was sitting on the couch, her legs tucked under her, her arms wrapped around her. He crumpled some newspapers and laid a fire in the fireplace. The flames crackled and the kindling caught fire and the flames burned once again in his blood. He tried to ignore her, but that was impossible. Deep worry lines were etched in her forehead. He was worried, too. Worried about Morgan, worried about Laurie and worried about the apple crop.

He glanced at Laurie and willed her to look at him. He wanted to tell her, reassure her... But when her gaze met his he forgot what he was going to say. Something snapped inside his head and all the tension, the worry, the anxiety over Morgan burst like a bombshell.

She got to her feet and came to him like a sleepwalker, her gaze tangled with his. And she didn't stop until she'd walked into his arms. Her arms tightened around him and her breath was warm against his cheek.

"Cooper," she said. "This is crazy."

He turned her face with his thumb under her chin. "Here's to craziness," he said under his breath.

She smiled, an achingly lovely smile. "Another one of your Scottish toasts?"

He trailed his lips down her throat. The desire built and threatened again just as it had that night at the talk. Did she feel it? Did she want it too?

Her heart was beating wildly against his. That was all he needed. He cupped her head with his broad palms and angled her mouth for a deep, profound kiss that went on and on and on. She poured herself into it, seeking release from the hours of worry, of tension. Reaching out to take and to give and to take again.

Laurie knew that if no phone rang and no baby cried there would be no stopping her this time. If she couldn't have all of Cooper, she'd take what she could get. If he wanted to make love with her, she wanted it more. If he walked out tomorrow, then she'd have tonight. She knotted her fingers behind his head and molded her lips to his hot hungry mouth. She wanted him close, closer. She wanted to lose herself, to forget the past, not worry about the future.

She wanted to do it here in front of the fire. On that hand-woven Indian rug. She wanted the heat from the flames on her bare skin, wanted to see the flames reflected in his dark eyes along with the passion she'd only glimpsed before. He groaned deep in his throat and she knew he wanted it, too.

When he ran his hands under her shirt warming her skin she sighed deeply. "Your skin is like silk," he murmured against her ear. His fingers slipped under her bra and unhooked it and she trembled. The heat built low in her belly, while her head floated somewhere above her body, too light, too dizzy.

Cooper molded her breasts to fit his hands, marvelled at their size and their weight and thought he might die if he couldn't possess her soon. But first he had to say something, something that was simmering in his mind like the chicken curry on the stove. He took her by the hands and brought her to her knees on the rug in front of the fire. The firelight turned her hair to gold, her skin the color of honey. God, how he wanted her, all of her, not just her body, but her mind and her soul.

He leaned back against the couch and took a deep breath. She was watching him, breathing hard, gripping the folds of the rug in her hands.

"You must know how I feel about you," he said gruffly.

She shook her head.

"No, how could you?" He stared into the flames. Wishing he could just make love to her and that would solve everything. But it wouldn't. "I've always thought I'd never love again...after what happened." He glanced at her and her eyes were on his, waiting, watching. There was an ache in his heart, a giant lump in his throat. It was guilt and he had to get around it. "I thought I couldn't, I knew I *shouldn't*. But here I am, falling in love again." Her eyes widened. "With you." He took both hands and ran his fingers through his hair. "I don't know where it's going. I don't want to tell you it's going to lead to happily ever after...because I don't know that." He stopped and shook his head. "Am I making any sense?"

"I think so," she whispered.

"I can't stand to see you hurt again, Laurie. But I want to give it . . . us . . . a chance. To see if something could work out between us. Something real and permanent. Right now, I think it can. But maybe it's just lust, sex, chemistry." He rubbed his forehead. "What do you think?"

She licked her lips. "Yes, I think there's a lot of that going on, what you said," she said, her cheeks tinted rose, her hair gold. "I'd . . . I'd be willing to take a chance. I mean, I'm a big girl. I've been hurt before and I'll probably be hurt again. But I recover. I have a lot of resilience." She smiled and he felt tears spring to his eyes. She'd take a chance on him. He didn't deserve it. He didn't deserve her. But when was it against the law to want something you didn't deserve?

He took her in his arms and held her. The warmth of her body infusing him with hope and strength. "In the meantime I'm going to try my level best not to get you into bed or onto any more carpets because somehow you cloud my mind and I want to think clearly." She whispered "okay" in his ear and he continued. "It's going to take all my willpower, but I really am going to try."

"It's a deal," she said, pulling back and holding out her hand.

He pressed her fingers to his lips. And tasted sugar and spice and all that was good about her. He helped her to her feet. They went to the couch together and sat next to each other, her head on his shoulder and watched the flames dance in front of them. And as the afternoon wore on, they took turns walking down the hall to look at Morgan, to pick her up, to give her a drink, and to walk her back and forth until she fell into a restless sleep again.

Laurie didn't ask Cooper to take turns with her. She didn't ask him if he was sure about his feelings and about wanting to take a chance on love again. She didn't need to. She could see it in his eyes, feel it in his touch when he brushed by her in the hallway or in the kitchen. She was afraid to think about it, afraid to hope, but being human, she did anyway.

They continued that way for the next two days. And nights. Laurie would hear Morgan cry in the night and she'd stagger to her feet and into the nursery to find Cooper there ahead of her, pacing back and forth beside the crib with Morgan in his arms, or sitting in the rocking chair holding her until she fell asleep. Laurie was too tired and too worried about Morgan to realize how strange it was. How incredible that this man who only recently professed to not want any type of emotional involvement with women and children was now in the middle of caring for a sick baby and contemplating a future with a woman he barely knew.

The apples suffered during this time. Between the two of them, they were only able to pick in short bursts, and then rush back to check on Morgan. When the skies cleared, Morgan's head cleared, too. And the deer cleared out. One morning Laurie went to the barn to see what she could use for a roadside stand. She'd been intrigued by the idea ever since that family came looking for one. And now that Morgan wasn't sick, she wanted something to do, something that would take her mind off Cooper and their new relationship.

It was awkward, knowing that he was trying out his new feelings, and knowing that she would follow him to the ends of the world's rivers if he said the word. The word was love, and he hadn't said it yet. Oh yes, he said he was 'falling in love,' but that didn't mean he was there yet. Or that he'd ever get there. And what about children? He hadn't mentioned taking a chance on children. And she understood. She really did. If she'd lost a child she'd be too heartbroken to try again.

It was going to be hard to leave Morgan. Even though she slobbered all over Laurie's clean shirts, kept her jumping with her demands for attention, Laurie would miss the little arms wrapped around her neck, her sweet baby smell, her cooing and her toothless smiles. Taking care of Morgan had been an eye-opening experience, one she wouldn't have missed for the world. Especially if she never had children of her own.

With the scrap wood and the wooden horses in the barn she and Cooper made a roadside stand and together they hauled boxes of apples to the road. They posted signs on the power poles along the road. An old scale served to weigh the apples and they kept the cash in a cigar box.

The customers who came admired the farm and Morgan in her miniature overalls playing in her playpen. The air was cool and crisp, the apples crisp and delicious. Laurie exchanged a proud smile with Cooper after a successful Saturday. The money box was full, the apple bins were empty and Morgan was content. What more could anyone want? Laurie knew the answer to that.

Chapter Nine

"Today is another one of those days that makes you want to go out and buy apples, isn't it?" Laurie asked Cooper on Sunday morning as she dressed Morgan in a plaid shirt and denim coveralls that almost matched Laurie's own work clothes.

Cooper opened the living room window and inhaled the clear fresh autumn air. "You're right," he said. "In fact here comes somebody now. She can't even wait for the stand to open. She's coming right up to the front door." He closed the window and went to the door. "What can we do for you?" he asked the long-legged teenager who stood on the Welcome mat with a backpack and a cheerful expression on her freshly scrubbed face.

Her eyes widened. "I'm Lucy the baby-sitter. Mrs. Lundgren hired me. You know, the cruise?"

Cooper turned to Laurie. "Do you know anything about a baby-sitter?"

Laurie wrinkled her nose. "No...wait a minute. She *did* say something...about going on a cruise. Then in all the excitement I forgot."

While Laurie went to the kitchen to check Gretel's calendar, Lucy came into the living room, made herself at home by playing a game of peekaboo with Morgan. It was clear they had a long-standing, friendly relationship, Cooper thought as he watched the game from across the room. When Laurie came back into the room she was holding a pair of tickets in her hand.

"These were pinned to the bulletin board," she explained. "Two tickets to a cruise on the Niagara River. I think they were for Gretel and me. She must have gotten her dates mixed up."

Lucy looked up from the floor where she was sitting with Morgan. "My mom and dad went on that cruise. For their anniversary. They said it was great."

"Do you want to go on a cruise?" Laurie asked Cooper.

"Sure, but..."

"What about the apples, the stand, the customers, the business...what about Morgan?"

Cooper shrugged. "Morgan seems to be okay. It's a shame to waste the tickets." He surveyed her carefully, noting the tiny lines etched in her forehead. "And you need a break."

She surveyed him just as carefully. "So do you."

He smiled. "Let's go for it."

Laurie smiled back, feeling a rush of excitement. She told herself it wasn't as if they were sailing to the Caribbean for two weeks. It was just brunch on the river. But that didn't slow the quickening of her pulse. If she were sensible she'd forget the tickets and go right back to the stand, haul the apples, sell apples and make money for Gretel. But she could almost hear Gretel's voice telling her to go, to enjoy. But what if Gretel knew that she was falling in love with a man who really didn't want to get married again? Then what? She might tell her to stay, stay. To send him away before it was too late. As if it wasn't already too late.

Cooper went to change clothes. Laurie explained Morgan's schedule to Lucy, then went down the hall to the master bedroom to find some cruise clothes. A half an hour later they were walking out the front door with the directions to the Buffalo Harbor in hand.

As they walked to the car Laurie stole a glance at Cooper. In his gray slacks, navy blazer and blue oxford shirt, the man was incredibly handsome. But it wasn't the clothes. He was equally good-looking with his wet, dirty shirt plastered to his skin. She tried to keep her eyes on the road as they drove through the countryside, but she couldn't help looking at Cooper, studying his profile, memorizing it, afraid that one day he'd be gone.

She smoothed the pale pink silk of her dress, thankful she'd packed it alone with a matching sweater. She felt ten pounds lighter today without a crate of apples in her arms, or a baby on her hip. The silk rustled against her skin, her hair fell loose and brushed her shoulders. She felt—how was it? young and single again? Or married and out with her husband? She wasn't sure which.

At Buffalo Harbor the *Niagara Princess* was waiting at the dock, white and sleek and streamlined, with brightly colored flags flying from her upper deck. Laurie felt a shiver of anticipation as they walked up the gangway. The purser in his white jacket welcomed them aboard just like on the Love Boat.

Laurie told herself this was just a river. Just a brunch that would last a few hours and then be over. But she couldn't shake the picture of a cabin for two, a porthole, romantic ports of call and Cooper... Cooper under the sun, Cooper under the moon. Cooper dining across the table in a well-tailored tux, Cooper in her bed, making love to her all night long. As she stood at the rail her face flamed. She told herself she'd seen too many movies. The band struck up "Anchors Away." The horn section finally blew Laurie out of her trance. Someone above them threw confetti from the upper deck. In another moment she was waving goodbye to a handful of dockworkers with Cooper's shoulder pressed against hers.

Even if they were going for a week she didn't think she could be any happier than she was right that moment with Cooper at her side, so warm, so solid, so real.

"Ever been on a cruise before?" Cooper's voice interrupted her reverie as the harbor receded in the distance.

"No, but I always wanted to go. It was nice of Gretel to plan this. I'm just sorry she can't be here." Liar.

She hadn't given Gretel a thought for hours. And she had a feeling that Gretel, with her romantic matchmaking nature, would want Laurie to take the cruise with Cooper. But not if she knew it might never work out, that there was only a possibility of a happy ending. Gretel wanted Laurie to find the same happiness she had. Was this really the way to do it? Laurie was filled with fears and doubts.

She was afraid Gretel would tell her to cut her losses and move on. She would move on, too, but not just yet. Not until Gretel came home. Not until the cruise was over. A river breeze blew her hair across her cheek and she looked away from the city skyline and into Cooper's blue eyes.

He gazed at her, his eyes brimming with a longing that matched her own.

She took a deep breath. "What about you?" she asked. "Have you ever been on a cruise?"

He shook his head. "But I like being on the water... away from it all."

"Away from apples," she suggested.

"From apples and customers... I don't take vacations, but if I did..." He looked at the reflections in the dark blue river water. "It might not be a bad idea." He reached for her hand and held it tightly.

"You might get bored," she suggested, watching a flock of shorebirds and allowing the warmth of his fingers to spread through her body.

"Not with you along."

She held her breath. She'd been holding it since the day he told her he would give it—them—a chance. And yet she couldn't help but hope, couldn't help the smile that tilted the corners of her mouth. When she finally met his gaze, she couldn't let go.

Something passed between them at that moment, an exchange, an understanding, almost too fleeting to register. And her hopes soared.

"Well," he said at last in a voice unusually low, "let's look around." Hand in hand they explored the decks of the clipper. From bridge to bow, from port to stern. They tried on their bright orange life jackets as instructed by the captain. Cooper fastened the ties for Laurie, his hands grazing the silk that covered the swell of her breasts. For a long moment they stood facing each other, life jacket to life jacket until the loudspeaker over their heads announced the lifeboat drill was over and brunch was being served.

Cooper helped Laurie out of her jacket, his hands lingering on her shoulders, and they went into the dining room. A white-jacketed waiter poured champagne and placed little dishes of fresh fruit in front of them—last-of-the-season strawberries, blueberries and kiwi fruit.

"It seems strange not to reach over and feed Morgan," Laurie mused as she sipped her champagne.

"Or to bend over and get her toys from the floor," he added.

"She's a lot of trouble," Laurie said.

"Not always."

"She's better lately. Maybe she's getting used to us or we're getting used to her."

"Just before we leave," Cooper noted. "When Gretel and Steve are almost home."

"Yes. Only a few more days." And then a decision—some kind of decision. Would they split up or stay together?

"How long will you be around?" she asked casually.

"I'm not sure. I have a final report to write. And I'm waiting to hear from the agency I work for."

"Where will they send you?"

He shrugged. "It could be anywhere, the Nile River or the Amazon. Anyplace where they have rivers, water and dams."

She realized he hadn't asked her to go with him.

"Do you like traveling?" she asked, watching the bubbles burst in her champagne.

"Of course, or I wouldn't do it. Don't you?"

"Of course, or I wouldn't have joined the airline. I'll miss my travel benefits."

It seemed they'd been to many of the same places in the world. And some of them at the same time. It gave Laurie a funny feeling in her stomach to think of passing Cooper on the streets of New Orleans or Timbuktu and never noticing him. But she would have noticed, she thought. She would have noticed that face, those deep-set eyes that changed from sea blue to navy, just as they were doing now.

He told her what his favorite places were and she either agreed or disagreed as they worked their way through a five-course meal, hardly noticing what they ate, they were so engrossed in each other. Over coffee their conversation dwindled. Afterward they walked out on deck, hands lightly twined together, deliberately casual. The music from the orchestra wafted out through the glass doors onto the deck as they stood gazing at the wilderness of Grand Island, a haven for wildlife and native vegetation. Laurie thought that she might never have been so happy in her whole life.

"Except for the bridges, this place hasn't changed since the French explorers paddled through here in their canoes," Cooper remarked.

"Imagine seeing the Falls for the first time," she said dreamily. "What must they have thought?"

"What did *you* think?" he asked, pulling her tightly against his side, her hip against his, his breath warm against her cheek.

"Me?" She kept her eyes on the park that lined the river on the Canadian side. "I was too worried about my keys at the bottom of the gorge to think of the spectacle in front of my eyes. I guess you saw the whole thing."

"Yes." There was a long silence while he breathed in the scent of her hair and tried to remember that day, that first day. What if he'd left the troll on the floor of the hotel lobby instead of picking it up? What if he'd ignored the crying coming from the lobby and continued on with his meeting? Where would he be right now?

He realized with a jolt how lonely he'd been, how flat his life was until she came into his hotel room, and into his life with her warmth, her energy, her love and her loyalty. She'd make somebody a great wife. And a great mother. He only had to see her with Morgan to know that. The old familiar pain twisted his heart as he thought about the past. But he kept Laurie pinned close to him because he couldn't let her go. Not now.

Not ever. She could be his wife, the mother of his children. All he had to do was say the words. . . .

He lifted her hair from the back of her neck and kissed the sensitive skin behind her ear, intoxicated by the touch and the scent of her. She turned to face him, her mouth inches from his, her lips parted, her eyes glazed with desire. He looked around the empty deck then back at her. His heart rocketed against his chest. He'd have to be blind to miss the invitation there in her eyes. Slowly, deliberately, he lowered his head and captured her lips with his.

She slipped her hands around his neck and answered his kiss with one of her own. One that left no doubt about how she felt. One that said she knew what she wanted and she wanted him. Beneath that cool, calm exterior was a warm, passionate woman. He knew that; he'd known it since the first night in the nursery of the stone house. Since their first kiss. But that was child's play compared to this one. This one sizzled, singed him to the core. Burned its way into his subconscious. And made him want more. She gave him more; her mouth molded to his.

His back was wedged against the railing, his hands braced against the wide polished wood. The sound of the waves slapping against the side of the boat kept time with his heart and with hers. A corner of his mind wondered if anyone else was on deck. He didn't care.

A deep ache started deep down in his gut and now consumed him. Laurie's lips parted and his tongue met hers in an eager and passionate dance. And he wanted more. He wanted everything. He desired her, needed her, but did he deserve her? He'd had one chance for happiness in this life and he'd blown it. Chances like that didn't come around twice. And yet... She was giving him a second chance. His mind was in turmoil. He broke the kiss and turned away from her.

Laurie bit her tongue to keep from crying out. From asking what was wrong. She knew what was wrong. She wrapped her arms around her waist as if to protect herself from the cold, but it was the truth she didn't want to face. The truth was he didn't want to get over the past. He wanted to live and relive it.

Cooper thought it was wrong to move on. Maybe it was. How did she, Laurie Clayton, presume to know what was best for him? Maybe all he needed was the right woman to help him start over. Maybe she wasn't that woman. Obviously not or he wouldn't refuse to even talk about it with her. She shivered in the cool afternoon breeze and with her head held high she walked away from him without a backward glance and went in to the enclosed deck. Only a fool would let her heart be broken twice by men who didn't want her. And Laurie was no fool. Or was she?

They spoke only a few more words during the rest of the cruise. Knowing he was still thinking things over, Laurie tried to avoid Cooper, by making polite conversation with a couple celebrating their fiftieth anniversary, then chatted with another couple who'd just gotten engaged. Nothing like a cruise for romance, she thought ironically. For everyone but her. She gazed out at the scenery and counted the minutes until their return at the dock back in Buffalo.

They walked in strained silence to the parking lot, Laurie's legs wobbling as if she'd been at sea for a week instead of a few hours. Then they got into Cooper's car and began the drive home. Laurie felt more like she'd been shipwrecked than on a luxury cruise. She was a big girl, she told herself, capable of serving drinks and dinners to 250 passengers without missing a beat and capable of caring for an eight-month-old baby and running an apple orchard on the side. Of course, having Cooper's help made it easier, but she could have managed by herself.

And she'd gotten over one disastrous love affair and if need be she could get over another. As soon as she knew where she stood. She stole a look at Cooper's profile as he drove. His expression was grim, his mouth clamped shut. It could be because of her, or it could have had more to do with the car in front of him who was alternately slowing down and speeding up.

In any case his mouth was clamped shut. The warm, sensuous lips that had kissed her breathless only a few hours ago were only a memory. He didn't look at her. His eyes were glued to the traffic jam ahead of them. Suddenly he jammed his foot on the brake, the car behind them slammed into Cooper's rear bumper. Laurie threw her arms forward to brace herself but her head hit the dashboard with a thump. Pain shot through her head and everything went black.

Cooper swore violently. "Laurie, my God, Laurie." He pulled her back from the dashboard, his heart pounding like a jackhammer. What had he done? He should have seen she wasn't wearing her seat belt. He should have pulled off to the shoulder and waited for the traffic to clear. He should have taken another route...should have, *would have,* could have all danced around in his brain while he begged and pleaded with Laurie to speak to him, to give him a sign she was all right. He knew she was alive, but she was limp in his arms, a huge welt forming on her forehead.

In the background coming closer there were sirens, patrol cars, an ambulance. He gave his name a dozen times, as well as her name, and they finally lifted her out of the car, onto a stretcher and into the ambulance. She looked so pale and shaken he was jerked back to that other time, the other tragedy and as he made his way in his dented car through the city streets to the hospital he knew. He knew with bone-crushing certainty he couldn't live through another death of somebody he loved. Not ever again.

At the hospital he waited outside the emergency room, pacing back and forth, pausing only to telephone the baby-sitter and tell her they'd be late. Finally the doctor came out and took him aside. Cooper waited, holding his breath.

"Mrs. Clayton is going to be fine. In fact she's chomping at the bit to get out of here. Asking for you, if you're Cooper, talking non-stop to the nurses about getting back to Morgan."

"She's okay, really okay?" he demanded.

"She suffered a minor concussion. But aside from a nasty bump on the head, she's all right. She should rest, of course, no strenuous activity for twenty-four hours. Is that understood?"

Cooper nodded, unable to speak, unable to believe Laurie was really all right until he saw for himself. And in a few minutes he did. They wheeled her out in a wheelchair, but she insisted on getting up out of it when she saw him. The white bandage accentuated the pallor of her skin, but her eyes looked bright and alert. Cooper was shaking, but Laurie seemed calm. He put his hands on her shoulders and looked anxiously into her eyes.

"Cooper, I feel so silly. All this fuss for nothing. I mean I've blacked out before and no one called an ambulance. Let's go home. I bet poor Lucy is worried sick by now."

"No, I called her," he said, taking her arm and walking out the emergency door. He still couldn't believe she was alive, not only alive but walking and talking and acting as if nothing had happened.

But it had. He'd almost lost her. If he'd been going any faster, if his car had been any smaller or lighter... He tried to act calm for Laurie's sake, but inside he felt like he was coming apart, that it was only his jacket and pants and shirt that were holding him together.

"You know, I always wear my seat belt," she said fastening it tightly across her chest. "But for some reason I'd unbuckled it...I know, to fix my shoe. The heel felt loose..."

She was chattering. It was nerves. She wasn't as calm as she would like him to believe. He wasn't either. But it affected him in the opposite way. He couldn't speak. Couldn't think of anything to say. She was having a delayed reaction and so was he. The more she talked, the quieter he became.

When he pulled up in front of the stone farmhouse, Laurie scarcely waited for the car to stop before she jumped out. He wanted to help her, but he knew it was important for her to prove she could do it herself. That she wasn't hurt. But he knew better. Though it was only a bump on the head, she'd been shaken, frightened, and needed some TLC.

Instead of Lucy at the door it was Gretel. Cooper watched them shriek and embrace from the driveway, feeling like an outsider. He heard Gretel exclaim over Laurie's head, saw her take her by the hand into the house and he knew she'd be taken care of. She didn't need him any more. And he knew he'd come *that* close to losing her. It didn't matter what the doctor said, he'd heard the squeal of the brakes, the sickening thud of her head against the windshield, the sound of the sirens.

And he *knew,* this time he knew it was his fault. He also knew he was wrong. He'd never completely re-covered from his wife's death and he never would. This accident today brought it all back with devastat-ing clarity. And showed him what he risked if he dared love again. He stood frozen at the front door and watched Gretel hover over Laurie like a mother hen.

Gretel had Laurie lying flat on the couch with a cold compress on her head and a blanket wrapped around her while she sat next to Laurie watching her with a worried look on her face.

But Laurie played down the seriousness of the crash. He heard her say she'd been careless and de-served a bump on the head. Then Laurie asked Gretel why she'd come back early.

"We got homesick. I mean Steve got homesick," Gretel explained. "Couldn't stand it another day without seeing Morgan..."

"Morgan!" Laurie leaned forward on one elbow but Gretel eased her back down onto the cushions.

"Sleeping," Gretel explained. "What a job you've done for us here! Morgan looks great. Anyway we're home and it's so good to be back." She looked around the room, her eyes lingering on the ashes in the fireplace and the wall hangings.

"Where's Steve?" Laurie asked, closing her eyes as the room spun around her.

"In the orchard. After he saw Morgan, he had to check on the apples." She looked up. "Oh, my gosh, it's Cooper, the hermit, the recluse. I can't believe my eyes. Do we owe you or what? Wait till Steve sees you're really here." She stood and hugged him.

Laurie's eyes were only tiny slits by then and everything was blurry, but she thought Cooper was standing over her looking down at her. But she closed her eyes for a moment and when she opened them, he was gone.

She didn't protest when Gretel put her to bed in the guest room after dispensing two of the pills the doctor had given her. She fell asleep with the scent of Cooper all around her. The sheets, the blanket surrounded her with a mixture of leather and soap and all outdoors. She snuggled deep into the bed he'd been sleeping in and fell into a dreamless sleep.

In the morning her head hurt like crazy but she felt wide awake and alert. She stood and stretched, realizing she was in a pair of Gretel's flannel pajamas. Then she tiptoed down the hall and into the living room. There was a pile of blankets on the couch and a pillow. And Cooper was standing on the front porch.

From the back she could see he'd slept in his clothes. She opened the front door and stepped outside in the cool fresh air. He turned and looked at her.

"How do you feel?" he asked anxiously.

"Fine." She looked at his wrinkled shirt, his tousled hair, and his bloodshot eyes. "Going somewhere?"

"As a matter of fact..."

"You're leaving, aren't you?" she said, feeling her cheeks flame. He took her by the elbows and eased her into the porch swing. "Were you even going to say goodbye?" she demanded, shaking him off.

"Of course I was," he said stiffly. "I have to apologize."

"For what? Not fastening my seat belt for me? I'm an adult, you know. I take responsibility for my own actions."

"You don't know how I felt..." he began.

"Let me guess," she sputtered. "You felt guilty, you felt it was happening all over again, the fear, the anxiety, the danger and the possibility that I might be killed just like..."

"Stop it," he said angrily. "You don't know, you *can't* know unless you've been through it."

"All right. All right," she admitted. "I don't know and I hope I never will. But I *do* know that you've suffered enough. You've felt enough guilt to last a lifetime. But you've got a lifetime ahead of you to live, to love again. If you'll just give yourself permission to take a chance on happiness. Of course something terrible could happen to you, to me, to anyone. But you can't go on expecting it, worrying about it, planning for it and dreading it. It's like a shadow over your life and..." Her head was throbbing and she was running out of arguments. He wasn't listening anyway.

"I appreciate your concern," he said between stiff lips. "I know what you think because it's what Steve thinks and what Gretel thinks. Go ahead and say it, you think I'm afraid to take a chance on love. You think I'm a coward." He loomed over her in the swing, his powerful form tense with bottled up frustration.

"Yes," she said quietly, "I think you're a coward."

He backed away from her then, his eyes as cold as ice. As true as the words were, she wished she could snatch them back. But he turned and stomped down the steps, went to his car and drove away without a backward glance.

Laurie slumped back in the swing, shaking like an autumn leaf. It was over. She should have know she never had a chance. But she'd hoped, she'd dreamed, she'd prayed... And now he was gone. With her words ringing in his ears. "A coward." Why did she have to say it? Because he'd asked for it. He deserved it. He *was* a coward, afraid to live, afraid to love. And she was better off without him.

That's what Gretel said later at breakfast. "You're better off without him, Laurie."

"I know, I know," Laurie said between bites of hot buttered toast. "But..."

"But what? He's got so much to give, so much to share...he's so kind, so sweet, so sexy. Is that what you were going to say?"

Laurie smiled, the first smile in such a long time. "No, that's not what I was going to say. I was going to say he's so pig-headed, domineering, stubborn, impossible..."

"True, true," Gretel acknowledged as she refilled Morgan's juice cup. "The good thing is you're over your pilot."

Laurie set her cup of herbal tea down. "How did you know about him?"

"Your sister called me last summer. She told me."

"Good grief, can't a person have any secrets?" Laurie asked mildly.

"Not around here," Gretel said, wiping Morgan's mouth. "Anyway we got you over that hangup and after your head heals, you'll be ready to face the world again with a brand-new outlook."

"If you say so," Laurie said, staring out the window at the bare branches of the apple trees. Yes, she'd gotten over Roger, only to find herself in love with Cooper, a man just as impossible as the last. Was that progress?

"You're sure you're okay?" Gretel asked with a worried frown. "You really weren't hurt in the crash?"

"Of course not," Laurie said with as bright a smile as she could muster. She couldn't spoil Gretel's return by moping around. "I really had a wonderful time here while you were gone," Laurie added earnestly.

"Sure you did. Picking apples, taking care of a teething baby and being subjected to the world's worst grouch," Gretel said.

"Cooper? Cooper's not a grouch," Laurie protested quickly. Maybe too quickly.

"Really?" Gretel asked, watching her friend out of the corner of her eye. "You could have fooled me. He hardly said two words at dinner last night. The dinner you slept through. Then he took off before breakfast, without saying a word. I don't call that exactly being sociable."

"I know what you mean. But honestly, Gret, he has good reasons."

"Such as?" Gretel asked with a raised eyebrow.

"You know about his wife and how she died."

"I also know it was two years ago."

"And he didn't take off without a word. I saw him this morning. I think he feels terrible about what happened."

"What happened?"

"Well, uh, nothing really."

"Does he know how you feel about him?" Gretel asked.

"I'm afraid so. Needless to say it's not mutual."

"Hmm."

Laurie waited, but Gretel didn't elaborate. And she wouldn't hear of Laurie taking off for California just because she and Steve came home early. "Tomorrow

Steve takes over the orchard and you and I take up where we left off.''

''I ought to be getting back to California. Mandy's baby is due fairly soon, you know.'' And everything about the orchard only reminded her of Cooper. This kitchen, the fireplace in the living room, the guest bedroom.

''Yes, but I also know you haven't had a real vacation. I promised to show you around and I'm going to do it.''

''Would two more days cover what we've missed?'' Laurie asked, hoping she could put up a cheerful front that long.

''I guess so,'' Gretel said with an exaggerated pout. And so they packed everything into those last two days, tea at the Olde English Hotel, the natural history museum and the harvest festival. And then it was time to go. Laurie said goodbye to Steve at the house, then Gretel and Morgan drove her to the airport. Gretel thanked her and she thanked Gretel. Laurie didn't cry, though she knew she was also saying goodbye to Niagara Falls and Cooper Buckingham at the same time as she said goodbye to her dear friend. Then she turned to the baby.

''I'll miss you, Morgan,'' Laurie told her goddaughter. She pressed her cheek against the baby's face and blinked back a tear. But the real tears came later as the plane took off and she gazed down at the orchards in the fall twilight, the mighty Niagara River and the spectacular Falls. She was getting away just in time. Another day and she might have called Cooper.

She might have told him she'd take him as he was. She didn't need children. She only needed him. She might have apologized for calling him a coward. She might have thrown herself at him. Told him she loved him. But it wouldn't have made any difference. And now at least she had her pride. For what it was worth.

Chapter Ten

Mandy Clayton watched her sister, Laurie, pace back and forth across the spacious living room of the Miramar Inn on the coast of northern California. The phone rang often with calls from prospective guests and each time it did Laurie held her breath while her sister answered it and then filled her reservation book with names and dates.

Finally Mandy looked up and, observing her sister closely, said, "Are you expecting a call by any chance?"

"No," Laurie blurted. "Why?"

"Because every time the phone rings you stop talking, lose your train of thought and we start all over again."

"How do you expect me to concentrate with you

talking on the phone, scribbling on your calendar and knitting your baby sweater all at the same time?"

"Of course you can't," Mandy said soothingly. "Now what were you saying about Gretel's baby?"

"She's adorable. Except when she's teething. Then she cries all the time."

Mandy examined the half-finished sweater with a practiced eye. "How awful. I hope *my* baby won't cry all the time."

"I'm sure it won't," Laurie assured her confidently.

"How did you ever manage with the baby and the apples and everything?"

"Mandy, I met someone," Laurie said suddenly.

Her sister dropped her knitting needles in her lap. "Why didn't you tell me?" she demanded.

"I *am* telling you. Although there's nothing to tell."

"Nothing? I don't believe you. Who is he? What does he do? Is it serious?"

"He's Cooper Buckingham. He worked at the Falls and no, it's not serious."

Memories danced before Laurie's eyes. The look in Cooper's eyes as he bent to kiss her, the lightning that illuminated his face the night of the storm, the kisses that would stay forever engraved in her soul.

"Not serious, you say. Then why have you been pacing around here like a caged tiger ever since you arrived?" Mandy said skeptically. "Why have you not heard anything I've said and why do you jump like a kangaroo every time the phone rings? Is he going to call you?"

"No, absolutely not. He doesn't know my number. He doesn't *want* to know my number. Have you heard enough?"

Mandy shook her head and picked up her yarn. "Not nearly enough. I want to hear everything. From the beginning."

Laurie sighed and looked out the window seeing rows of apple trees in her mind instead of the eucalyptus with their peeling trunks and fragrant leaves that framed Mandy's windows. "It all started when Morgan threw the car keys over the Falls."

Laurie told her the whole story. Or almost the whole story. She left out some private details. Details that were between her and Cooper only. Mandy turned on the lamps on the end tables, lit a fire in the fireplace and poured them each a glass of sherry. It was a weeknight and there were no guests to share it with. Mandy's husband was at a Rotary Club meeting in town.

"Wow," Mandy said, sipping her sherry. "I feel like I lead an awfully dull life."

"I'd trade it in a minute," Laurie said with an envious glance at her sister's round, expanding stomach under her colorful maternity smock. But deep down Laurie knew she wouldn't trade a minute of that time with Cooper—the way he smiled for example, the way he held Morgan. She'd hold on to those memories, because they were all she had.

"You'll get your chance," Mandy said, patting Laurie's hand. "In the meantime I'm glad to have you back. This is my busy season. I need you. Each week I get a little heavier and a little more tired."

Laurie gave her sister an affectionate look. "Even heavy and tired you have more energy than most people do." She sighed and leaned back against the cushions. "Mandy, what should I do?"

"Have a hot bath and go to bed."

"I mean with the rest of my life. I can't stay here with you, living in an apartment over the garage, growing as old and gray as little Brunhilde's aging auntie."

"You could, but you probably shouldn't. Let's see, you look great in a uniform, you're good with kids... Be a Girl Scout leader?"

Laurie choked on a laugh, which turned into a sob. "Don't be funny. I'm not in the mood."

"Sorry. I was just testing you. And you failed miserably. You are serious about this guy, aren't you?"

"No. Yes. I could be. I would be. But he doesn't want to get married. And he especially doesn't want to have children. He has a good reason."

"Don't they all," Mandy said dryly. "Haven't you heard that before?"

"But this is different," Laurie protested. "Cooper is different."

"Sure he is. I'd say you got away just in time. If he doesn't want to get married, what does he want, an affair?"

"No," Laurie said. But she wondered. Isn't that where they had been heading that night in the guest room? And who would have stopped it? Not her. She'd wanted him so much she'd forgotten about what was important to her. Yes, Mandy was right. She'd gotten away just in time.

Another day and she would have thrown herself at him. Would have forgotten about marriage and children and would have settled for an affair. Now, back in her sister's house, she realized that she had to hold out for what she wanted. But as she washed sheets and towels during the next few days, baked muffins and served sherry in the evening to guests so Mandy could rest, she was beginning to have second thoughts. If he walked in the door at that moment and asked her to take up where they'd left off what would she say?

From the kitchen window she stared out at the dark blue ocean in the distance. She reminded herself that the chance of that happening was less than zero. That Cooper was doubtless hard at work somewhere and thinking about nothing but how to divert water flow. And he was glad to get away from crying babies and women who couldn't cope in emergencies.

But Cooper was not only thinking about diverting the water flow. He'd tried diverting his thoughts from Laurie, but he couldn't. Instead he went to see Morgan, Steve and Gretel in the orchard. He said he'd come to bring Morgan a present, and he did bring her a small stuffed dog, but that wasn't all. He'd come to see the place where he'd last seen Laurie. He thought it might make him feel better. But it only made him feel worse.

He missed her. He was confused, he was depressed and he was lost.

"Laurie's gone," Gretel said after she'd invited him into the kitchen for a cup of coffee.

As if he didn't know. As if he didn't feel her loss deep inside his bones. "I know. I didn't come to see her." His eyes roamed the kitchen remembering the hamburgers, the chicken curry, the pancakes, her apple cake. But most of all remembering how she looked hovering over the stove, her cheeks pink with concentration, her eyes locked with his, the tension in the air. "I just wondered if you had her address," he said with a careless shrug as if it didn't really matter one way or another.

Gretel raised her eyebrows in surprise, but she opened a drawer and took out a piece of notepaper and wrote down the address of the Miramar Inn for him.

He put it in his pocket. "How is she?" he asked as Gretel poured two cups of coffee.

"I haven't heard from her since she left. She's probably busy at the inn, helping her sister. It's a beautiful spot. Perfect for R and R or a romantic weekend . . ."

"I meant how is Morgan," he said. He knew the Miramar Inn was beautiful and romantic. He didn't want to hear about it again.

"Morgan? She's fine. Taking a nap."

"I miss her," he blurted.

"Morgan?"

"No, Laurie."

Gretel nodded understandingly. "She's a special person. And she deserves the best."

Cooper knew she was looking at him over the rim of her cup. Probably thinking that he didn't fit the bill. She was probably right.

The thought of Laurie finding someone else, someone who'd give her everything she wanted caused him
to grip the edge of the counter so tightly it turned his
knuckles white. He looked around the kitchen again
at the bright yellow curtains and the natural pinewood counters. "You have a great life here," he said.

"But you have a pretty interesting life yourself," she
remarked.

"I used to think so, until... Well, it seems empty
now."

"What are you going to do?" she asked.

"Talk to Steve," he said.

She gestured toward the grove of trees behind the
house. "He's out there grafting."

Steve put his pruning shears down when he saw his
old friend, wiped his brow and held out his hand. "I
thought maybe you'd left," he said.

Cooper shook his head. "I had to say goodbye."

"Where're you off to?"

"Not sure. I've got several offers, some interesting
projects, but... I don't know."

"We appreciate what you did here, you know."

"I'm not sure Gretel does," Cooper said, staring off
into the bare trees.

"You know what she's thinking. She wanted something to happen with you and Laurie. I told her not to
push it. Why, did she say something to you?"

"No...no. It's just...if something happened to
Gretel and Morgan, could you ever fall in love again?
And if you did, would you do anything about it, or
would you stay faithful to their memory?" He leaned

back against a gnarled old apple tree and looked at Steve with intensity, waiting for his answer.

But Steve only shook his head. "I don't know. How could I know? My heart goes out to you," he said and his eyes filled with tears.

Cooper looked away. He hadn't meant for the conversation to take this turn. "I'm sorry. Forget I said that. It's just that I have no one else to ask. To talk to."

"All I can say is if I died I'd want Gretel to marry again and be happy. I wouldn't want her to suffer. To live her life alone. I'm sure you feel the same."

Cooper had the feeling he'd heard this all before. From Laurie. "Of course I do. But what if something happens? Now that I know how fragile life is, how temporary, I can't help thinking..."

"That it could happen again? I see what you mean. Because if it did..."

"I couldn't take it. It almost killed me the last time. The next time definitely would."

Steve studied his friend. "Do you love Laurie?"

Cooper nodded slowly. "That doesn't make it any easier."

"What, taking a chance again?"

"Yes. And to ask her to take a chance on me. What if I'm not capable of really loving again? Maybe I just think I'm in love with her. Maybe I've forgotten what it takes."

"You don't forget that kind of thing. Think of it this way. The more you love, the more love you've got to give. I swear I didn't know how to love a baby. I thought Gretel and I had it all, but she wanted a baby.

I told her we couldn't afford it, we needed her salary. I told her to wait. But she wouldn't wait. She wanted it *now*. And guess what, I love that little kid more than I could have imagined.''

Cooper watched Steve's eyes turn soft and his mouth curve into a smile and Cooper just stared at him. Was this the same guy whose ambition was once to date every girl on the whole campus and to raise as much hell as possible?

"Anyway," Steve said, picking up his shears and running his finger along the blade. "You've got more to give than any man I know. You had something great once. I know. But it's time to start over. You've spent two years getting over it and you've got to move on. Stop beating yourself up. It was a tragedy that happened. But it wasn't your fault. You've put yourself through hell and now you've got another chance. Not everybody gets another chance, and not everybody is smart enough to take it. Maybe it won't work out, but I saw how you looked at her, and I know you've got it bad. I think she feels the same, but you'll never know unless you get yourself out to California to that bed-and-breakfast, rent a room and stay there until you recover or she gives in."

Cooper swallowed the lump in his throat and nodded. He gripped Steve by the shoulder, shook his hand and walked around the house to his car. He should have said goodbye to Gretel, but he didn't trust his voice at that moment and he had things to do and miles to go.

* * *

On a brisk November day with the sheets and towels blowing in the wind from the clothesline behind the house, Laurie Clayton was on the telephone discussing the newspaper ad for her sister's bed-and-breakfast with the layout artist. Her sister was still in bed and Laurie hoped she'd stay there for a while and rest. Her due date was looming, her feet were swelling and her bladder was compressed to the size of a pea.

While Laurie was engaged in the discussion of how best to position the copy with the picture of the picturesque house on the edge of the sea, she heard a knock on the front door. She held her hand over the receiver and yelled, "Come in."

It was hardly likely to be a guest at this time of the morning, or she would have gone to the door herself and acted hospitable. It was probably just the repairman come to fix the drip in the kitchen sink.

But it wasn't. It was Cooper Buckingham standing in the doorway staring at her. Very, very slowly she hung up the phone and then she stood there behind her sister's cherrywood desk just staring back.

"I...uh...was wondering if there's a vacancy," he said.

"A vacancy," she repeated stupidly as her gaze wandered over his navy blazer, his striped shirt and creased slacks. "I believe so but I'll...have...to check."

"I've heard a lot about this place," he remarked, setting his overnight bag on the polished floorboards and looking around at the stone fireplace, the large comfortable chairs and the pictures of the Clayton family on the wall. "About how charming, how romantic it is."

Laurie skimmed through the appointment book, unable to locate the month of November to save her soul. The names of the months, the names of the guests all blurred in front of her eyes. "Are you alone?" she asked, closing the book shut and holding her breath.

"For now," he said.

"Because most people come with someone," she said. "Although it's not necessary. It's just that...as you say, it's so romantic."

"I understand there's sherry in the evening and fresh fruit."

"Cheese and crackers," she added inanely, when she wanted to scream out, What are you doing here? What do you want?

As if she'd spoken the words, he said. "I'm looking for someone, someone to share it with, the sherry, the fruit, my life..."

Laurie's knees shook so much at the sound of his voice that she had to sit down in the antique chair behind the desk. Had he really said "My life"? "How long would this be for?" she said, riffling through the pages again.

"Oh, something around forever," he said with a glint in his eye that made her heart pound. Oh, God, don't let me get my hopes up, she thought. Let me be as cool as he is.

At that moment her sister came down the stairs dressed in a bright maternity smock and hot pink leggings. Her hair was pulled back in a ponytail and she glowed like a picture-perfect mother-to-be.

"I thought I heard someone knock," she said, beaming, the perfect hostess even at nine months pregnant. "Is Laurie taking care of you all right?"

"Not really," he said with a sideways look at Laurie. "I've never been to a bed-and-breakfast before, but somehow I thought the welcome would be, I don't know, a little warmer."

Mandy looked back and forth between Laurie who by that time had turned almost scarlet with embarrassment and Cooper who was watching her.

"Mandy," Laurie protested, "this is Cooper Buckingham. Gretel and Steve's friend. He's just kidding, of course, about the welcome. I'm sure he didn't expect someone to throw their arms around him, I mean . . . after all . . ." He seemed to be amused at her discomfort, standing there watching her try to explain, so she walked out from behind the desk and turned to Mandy. "Since you're up, and you know what's what in the reservations book, I'll leave you to handle this. I've got, uh, something in the washer." Then with her chin at a defiant angle she strode purposefully from the room.

He didn't think he could walk into her sister's bed-and-breakfast and watch her fall to her knees in gratitude, did he? He didn't think she'd been sitting at that desk waiting for him to come. Maybe he thought her description of the place amounted to an invitation, when all she'd been doing was making conversation. Whatever he thought, she wasn't interested in finding out. She was determined to get over him, to cure herself forever of falling in love with the wrong men, and his coming here was not going to help her. It would just remind her of what she'd done wrong. Unless... unless...

Mandy slid her bulky body behind the desk to the chair that Laurie had just vacated. "Sit down, won't you?" she said to Cooper.

He took one of the straight-back chairs and faced Laurie's sister, searching for a family resemblance. When she smiled at him, he saw something in the curve of her lips that reminded him of Laurie. "I didn't really expect a warm welcome," he confessed. "I don't deserve one. Not from your sister."

Mandy nodded. "I heard all about it. She says you're not ready to get married. Not again. And especially not to have children. But Laurie's always wanted kids. More than I did. More than anybody. It's very important to her. So what I'm trying to say is that if you're here for the sea air, and the refreshments in the evening and the mints on the pillow, then I'm afraid there's no vacancy. I can't stand by and see her get hurt again."

"You and Laurie are very close," Cooper said, getting to his feet and pacing back and forth in front of the desk. "I envy that. I was an only child. I don't blame you for being protective of her. You don't want her to fall in love with the wrong man. I'm here to convince her I'm the right man. I've got to, because I don't want to live without her another day, not even another hour. She knows I love her, but she doesn't know I want to marry her and have kids and whatever else she wants. Now. Right away. Tomorrow. If she'll have me." He braced his arms on the desk. "Does that make sense to you?"

Mandy's eyes filled with tears. She nodded mutely, reached into the top drawer and held out the key to the large room at the top of the stairs with the view of the ocean usually reserved for honeymooners. "You'd better go find her," she sniffed, "before she gets lost under a pile of king-size sheets." She gestured to the back of the house.

Laurie hauled a large wicker basket filled with wet sheets out to the backyard, her muscles straining, her mind spinning. Why was he there? What were they doing in there? If he was staying, why didn't somebody tell her? When she looked through the windows she didn't see anyone. Had Mandy chased him away or forced a commitment out of him? Ever since Laurie had suggested her sister answer a personal ad in a magazine years ago, which had led to her marriage, Mandy had felt compelled to find Laurie a husband. But what if Mandy thought Cooper was another Roger? A man who wouldn't live up to his promises. If so she would have shown him to the door by now. Maybe he was on his way out at that very moment. She shouldn't have left them alone, not until she knew.

Laurie clamped a clothespin between her teeth and stretched a king-size sheet over the line. Mandy liked the bed linens to smell like fresh air and sunshine. Laurie sometimes wondered if it was really worth the trouble and if the guests really noticed. When the wind tore the sheet off the line and whipped it over her head, she swore softly and waved her arms wildly to disentangle herself.

It didn't do any good. She spun around in circles clutching the yards of material that wrapped around her body. In the background she heard the door to the patio open and slam shut, and then footsteps on the flagstones. A deep voice carried across the hedge that separated the patio from the lawn.

"The place has everything," the voice said. "A view and a resident ghost, too. Do you come out to meet new guests or are you a permanent fixture around here?"

Laurie dropped her arms to her sides and stopped struggling to get out from under the percale.

"What do you want?" she said in a muffled voice.

"I just want the answers to a few questions," he said, his voice getting louder, nearer.

"Don't come any closer," she warned. "or I'll put a spell on you."

"You already did," he said, taking her into his arms, sheet and all. "And I can't get out of it."

"Have you tried?" she asked, feeling his arms around her, the warmth of his body through the two-hundred-thread-count cotton.

"I've tried everything," he said fervently. "I've tried work and more work. I've tried returning to the scene of the spell. Nothing works. Got any suggestions?" he asked, finding her face under the sheet with his hands. With a tug he lifted the sheet over her head and tossed it to one side. Her hair had come loose from the rubber band that held it and brushed against her windburned pink cheeks. Her eyes, a rich caramel color, regarded him with wary interest.

"You could try throwing your car keys over the cliff," she suggested. "That sometimes works."

"That's how it all started," he recalled. "But then I couldn't leave."

"Were you planning to?" she asked.

"Not without you," he said, reaching into his pocket for the keys. "I went to see Steve and Gretel after you left." He rattled the keys in his hand. "They said you deserved the best. So if you want to keep looking... There are a lot of men in the foreign legion."

"But no women. You were right," Laurie admitted ruefully.

"Somewhere else then. But first I want to tell you that I can't forget the past. I'll always remember what I had and what I lost. But something happened when I met you. I fell in love with you, Laurie. Something I thought I never could do. You made me want to live again, to love again."

"To have children again?" she asked, pressing her hand to her heart, not daring to hope.

He smiled. "To have lots of children. With blond hair and eyes the color of autumn leaves."

"Some of them might look like you," she suggested, tears of happiness blurring her vision.

He swallowed hard and looked her in the eye. "That's the chance you'll have to take," he said, praying that she was willing to take the chance.

"I'll take it," she said softly.

"Then you'll come with me?" he asked, drinking in the sight of her with hungry eyes not daring to believe this was really happening.

"Where?"

"Wherever you want. Any more questions?" He held his breath. What if she'd changed her mind. Stopped caring. Stopped loving.

She searched his face for the answer to the most important question of all. In his eyes she saw the answer. She saw the love and trust and commitment she was looking for. But she wanted to hear it. She had to hear it.

"Laurie," he said, running his hands down her arms to clasp her hands in his. "You said it was time to forget. You said the past was over. But I couldn't let go. Until you left. Then I realized I loved you, needed you." She opened her mouth to speak but he shook his head. "No, wait. You said I'd make a wonderful father. I'm not so sure, but I'm going to try. But only if you'll be the mother of my children."

Laurie's eyes filled with tears. "Are you sure?" she whispered. His answer was to sweep her into his arms and carry her into the house and up to the room he'd reserved, where he convinced her beyond a doubt how sure he was.

Epilogue

Whistles blew, the band struck up "Anchors Away" and streamers flew from the upper deck of the SS Kungsholm bound for Hawaii, Samoa and Fiji from San Francisco. The blond woman in the pale green linen suit leaned over the railing and waved at her sister and brother-in-law who stood on the dock below blowing kisses. Then she turned to the man next to her in the blue blazer and gray slacks who was popping the cork on a bottle of champagne.

"It's even better than *Niagara Princess*," Laurie said, her eyes dancing with joy.

"Are you surprised?" Cooper asked.

"Surprised at the basket of fruit in the stateroom from Gretel and Steve? Surprised that Mandy came to see us off in her condition? And surprised to find us on a honeymoon cruise? Yes, yes and yes. It's everything I dreamed of."

"No Grand Island wilderness," he reminded her. "No houses along the river with beautiful lawns..."

"No," she agreed. "But there are tropical islands, midnight buffets, dancing till dawn..." She sighed blissfully. "And the stateroom with the enormous window."

"And the enormous bed," he added.

"Cooper Buckingham, are you trying to get me into bed before we've even sailed?" she asked in a shocked voice.

"Does that surprise you?" he asked with his arms around her waist, his dark blue gaze locked with hers.

"Nothing you do could surprise me," she said breathlessly.

But she was wrong. He surprised and delighted and loved her for fourteen days and fourteen nights at sea and then went on to a lifetime of surprises including a pair of twins with midnight blue eyes and identical impish senses of humor.

"What were the chances of this happening?" Laurie asked him several years later as they watched their children race along the beach below the Miramar Inn where they vacationed every year.

"One in a million," he answer with a broad smile and a kiss.

*   *   *   *   *

COMING NEXT MONTH

#1144 MOST WANTED DAD—Arlene James
Fabulous Fathers/This Side of Heaven
Amy Slater knew the teenage girl next door needed a sympathetic ear—as did her father, Evans Kincaid. But Amy found it hard to be just a *friend* to the sexy lawman, even though she'd sworn never to love again....

#1145 DO YOU TAKE THIS CHILD?—Marie Ferrarella
The Baby of the Month Club
One night of passion with handsome Slade Garret left Dr. Sheila Pollack expecting nothing...except a baby! When Slade returned and demanded marriage, Sheila tried to resist. But Slade caught her at a weak moment—while she was in labor!

#1146 REILLY'S BRIDE—Patricia Thayer
Women were in demand in Lost Hope, Wyoming, so why did Jenny Murdock want stubborn rancher Luke Reilly, the only man *not* looking for a wife? Now Jenny had to convince Reilly he needed a bride....

#1147 MOM IN THE MAKING—Carla Cassidy
The Baker Brood
Bonnie Baker was in Casey's Corners to hide from love, not to be swept away by town catch Russ Blackburn! Gorgeous, devilish Russ got under her skin all right...but could Bonnie ever risk love again?

#1148 HER VERY OWN HUSBAND—Lauryn Chandler
Rose Honeycutt had just blown out her birthday candles when a handsome drifter showed up on her doorstep. Cowboy Skye Hanks was everything she'd wished for, but would his mysterious past keep them from a future together?

#1149 WRANGLER'S WEDDING—Robin Nicholas
Rachel Callahan would do anything to keep custody of her daughter. So when Shane Purcell proposed a pretend engagement, Rachel decided to play along. Little did she know that the sexy rodeo rogue was playing for keeps!

They're the hardest working, sexiest women in the Lone Star State...they're

Annette Broadrick

The O'Brien sisters: Megan, Mollie and Maribeth. Meet them and the men who want to capture their hearts in these titles from Annette Broadrick:

MEGAN'S MARRIAGE
(February, Silhouette Desire #979)
The *MAN OF THE MONTH* is getting married to *very* reluctant bride Megan O'Brien!

INSTANT MOMMY
(March, Silhouette Romance #1139)
A *BUNDLE OF JOY* brings Mollie O'Brien together with the man she's always loved.

THE GROOM, I PRESUME?
(April, Silhouette Desire #992)
Maribeth O'Brien's been left at the altar—but this bride won't have to wait long for wedding bells to ring!

Don't miss the DAUGHTERS OF TEXAS—three brides waiting to lasso the hearts of their very own cowboys! Only from

 and ▼ *Silhouette* ROMANCE™

Bestselling author

RACHEL LEE

takes her Conard County series to new heights with

A CONARD COUNTY Reckoning

This March, Rachel Lee brings readers a brand-new, longer-length, out-of-series title featuring the characters from her successful Conard County miniseries.

Janet Tate and Abel Pierce have both been betrayed and carry deep, bitter memories. Brought together by great passion, they must learn to trust again.

"Conard County is a wonderful place to visit! Rachel Lee has crafted warm, enchanting stories. These are wonderful books to curl up with and read. I highly recommend them."
—*New York Times* bestselling author
Heather Graham Pozzessere

Available in March, wherever Silhouette books are sold.

STEP

INTO

THE  **WINNER'S CIRCLE**

A collection of award-winning books
by award-winning authors!
From Harlequin and Silhouette.

Available this April

TOGETHER ALWAYS

by DALLAS SCHULZE

Voted Best American Romance—
Reviewer's Choice Award

Award-winning author Dallas Schulze brings you the romantic
tale of two people destined to be together. From the moment
he laid eyes on her, Trace Dushane knew he had but one
mission in life...to protect beautiful Lily. He promised to save
her from disaster, but could he save her from himself?

Dallas Schulze is "one of today's most exciting authors!"
—Barbara Bretton

Available this April wherever Harlequin books are sold.

FIVE UNIQUE SERIES
FOR EVERY WOMAN YOU ARE...

▼ *Silhouette* ROMANCE™

From classic love stories to romantic comedies to emotional heart tuggers, Silhouette Romance is sometimes sweet, sometimes sassy—and always enjoyable! Romance—the way you always knew it could be.

SILHOUETTE® *Desire*®

Red-hot is what we've got! Sparkling, scintillating, *sensuous* love stories. Once you pick up one you won't be able to put it down...only in Silhouette Desire.

Silhouette SPECIAL EDITION®

Stories of love and life, these powerful novels are tales that you can identify with—romances with "something special" added in! Silhouette Special Edition is entertainment for the heart.

SILHOUETTE·INTIMATE·MOMENTS®

Enter a world where passions run hot and excitement is always high. Dramatic, larger than life and always compelling—Silhouette Intimate Moments provides captivating romance to cherish forever.

▼ SILHOUETTE YOURS TRULY™

A personal ad, a "Dear John" letter, a wedding invitation... Just a few of the ways that written communication unexpectedly leads Miss Unmarried to Mr. "I Do" in Yours Truly novels...in the most fun, fast-paced and flirtatious style!

HE'S NOT JUST A MAN,
HE'S ONE OF OUR

Fabulous Fathers

MOST WANTED DAD
Arlene James

Green hair? Music blasting at all hours? What's a single father of a teenage girl to do?

Asking the pretty lady next door for advice seemed like a good idea. Until Evans found out just how full of advice Amy Slater was—about his own lack of a wife!

This **Fabulous Father** is the best catch
This Side of Heaven!

Coming in April from

Silhouette

R O M A N C E™

FF496

Welcome to the

A new series
by Carol Grace

This bed and breakfast offers great views, gracious hospitality—and possibly even love!

You've already met proprietors Mandy and Adam Gray in LONELY MILLIONAIRE (Jan. '95). Now this happily married pair invite you to stay and share the romantic stories of how two other very special couples found love at the Miramar Inn:

ALMOST A HUSBAND—Carrie Stephens needed a fiancé—fast! And her partner, Matt Graham, was only too happy to accommodate, but could he let Carrie go when their charade ended?

AVAILABLE SEPTEMBER 1995

ALMOST MARRIED—Laurie Clayton was eager to baby-sit her precocious goddaughter—but she hadn't counted on Cooper Buckingham playing "daddy"!

AVAILABLE MARCH 1996

Don't miss these charming stories coming soon from

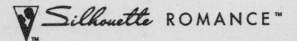